LIABILITY

A Romantic Thriller

SCREENPLAY

TODD CRAWSHAW

CrowsnestPublishing.com

When we cracked the genetic DNA code, opened the big Pandora's box, and it really did become possible to produce chimeras, my ears shot up. Having been brought up among the biologists and having followed various debates about ways to improve the human template and other debates about the true nature of our nature, I began seriously to wonder: What if? We hold in our hands a tool that is more powerful – for good or ill – than any we have wielded before.

—Margaret Atwood

FADE IN:

INT. CAFE, HWY 50, SIERRA MOUNTAINS - NIGHT

CORI VIDERI is seated at a window booth in a
mountain cafe. She is 27, unassuming yet fetch-
ing in a leather jacket, sweater and jeans. Her
expression is vacant. The cup of coffee in her
hand shakes. Her eyes tear up. She looks down.

In her palm she holds a cylindrical device the
size of a cigarette lighter, encased in metal.
Futuristic. Technical. She quickly places it
inside her purse.

CLOSE ON her eyes. A FLAME flickers inside her
pupils.

CLOSE ON an inverted FLAME becoming a MAN
wielding a gun.

Reflections in the dark cafe windows show a
WAITRESS on the floor, customers being robbed,
the GUNMAN approaching.

The gun barrel touches Cori's forehead.

                    GUNMAN
          Jewelry. Cash. Now.

Cori is yanked from the booth and brought to her feet.

The gunman looks her over.

                    GUNMAN
          You're coming with me, sweet thing.
               (lewd wink)
          Or were you hoping I'd put my bullet
          in you right here? You'd like that?

Cori maintains a calm demeanor. She secures a
tight hold on her purse. She refuses to budge
when her arm is yanked.

1

                    GUNMAN
        Don't fuck with me. Let's go. Move!

He FIRES his gun, SHATTERING a lamp. People SCREAM.

                    GUNMAN
        Anyone here want to be a dead hero?

INT. CLASSROOM - DAY (FLASHBACK)

Cori, 15, is gazing out a window. The teacher approaches.

                    TEACHER
        Videri. Caught daydreaming. Again.

                    CORI
        I wasn't.

                    TEACHER
        Then repeat the question I asked.

                    CORI
        What is liability?

                    TEACHER
        Amazing. Something I said actually
        got through to your brain.

The teacher smugly gestures with chalk in hand
to his class.

                    TEACHER
        Now, can you tell me its definition?

                    CORI
        Liability means...
                  (smiles)
        You possess the ability to lie.

Her classmates LAUGH. Chalk SNAPS between the
teacher's fingers.

INT. CAFE, SIERRA MOUNTAINS - SAME

The hammer of the gun CLICKS back a notch.

                    GUNMAN
          The fuck is wrong with you?

The gun barrel is pressed into her lips.

                    GUNMAN
          Don't tempt me. You think this is
          funny? You think this is all some
          fucking stupid joke?

                    CORI
          No. Just you.

His bag of loot is dropped on the table. He BACKHANDS
her. Cori rubs her cheek, snaps off her necklace.

                    CORI
          Here. Did you want this?

                    GUNMAN
          No. Just you.

                    CORI
          Then you'd better not look up.

The gunman glares back.

                    CORI
          Security camera.

                    GUNMAN
          There are no fucking cameras.

                    CORI
          Between the beams. To your right.
          Fine. Don't believe me.

The gunman hesitates but glances for the
nonexistent camera.

Cori KNEES him in the groin - JABS his throat - TORQUES his wrist - which releases the gun that DROPS from his hand.

Two men SCRAMBLE off the floor and POUNCE on the gunman.

Cori, still standing, is transfixed by something outside.

CUT TO: APPARITION of a woman watching from the parking lot.

A WAITRESS approaches Cori.

> WAITRESS
> Are you all right, Dear?

THE APPARITION DISPERSES INTO FADING PARTICLES OF LIGHT.

> CORI (O.C.)
> I'm fine, thanks.

> WAITRESS
> You're lucky to be alive.

Cori pulls out a five-dollar bill from her jeans.

> CORI
> I guess. Here. For the coffee.

> WAITRESS
> Keep it. We should be paying you.

> GUNMAN
> You'll die for that! Wait until I -

The gunman's mouth is sealed with duct tape. His hands and legs are strung together with fishing tackle.

A COWBOY in a hat approaches Cori and blocks her from leaving.

                    COWBOY
               (tips his hat)
     Police are on their way. You might
     want to stick around until then.

                    CORI
     We all saw what happened. Besides,
     I'm late for an appointment.

                    COWBOY
     At this hour?

                    CORI
     I'm an attorney. Here.

She pulls a business card from her pocket, hands
it to him.

                    COWBOY
     Mind if I ask you something?

                    CORI
     Ask.

                    COWBOY
     How'd you manage that?

                    CORI
     Manage what?

                    COWBOY
     Tricking him, and all the rest.

                    CORI
     It's a gift I have.

The cowboy questions her smile with a curious squint.

                    CORI
     Liability.

TITLE: NINE YEARS EARLIER

INT. ART CLASS, U.C. BERKELEY - NIGHT

A BLUR of colors comes into FOCUS to become a painting, which transitions into a live woman staring at herself in the mirror.

This is Cori at age eighteen. She has a haunted expression.

>   CORI (V.O.)
>   We mustn't judge God from this world.
>   It's just a study that didn't come
>   off. Only a master could make such a
>   blunder.
>   (a gun shot)
>   Vincent Van Gogh said that. When he
>   shot himself in a corn field, I think
>   he was aiming to shoot God.

A CAWING of crows fades into students TALKING from another room over a FLOW of water. Cori is at a wash basin cleaning paint brushes in a utility sink.

RED water flows from the faucet over her hands.

INT. LECTURE ROOM, COLLEGE CAMPUS - NIGHT

PROFESSOR NAUGHT, 45, a biochemist, presides over a small group of 12 students. Images are projected on a screen.

>   NAUGHT
>   Each person holds the potential for
>   greatness. Yet it goes unrealized.

INSERT - PREHISTORIC CAVE DRAWINGS ON A WALL.

>   NAUGHT (V.O.)
>   Plato conceived of us being chained
>   inside a cave viewing projections on
>   a wall. A distorted reality. Being
>   misguided by these specters.

He points to an illustration of DNA's double helix.

                    NAUGHT
          Darwin spoke of evolutionary chains
          that bind us from within. Spiraling
          codes that contain more phantoms.
          There is truth embedded in these
          genetic links, but also blinders to
          restrict us. Limitations that I will
          remove. So that your minds can
          clearly see this face we call God.

He takes a drink of water and holds forth the
empty glass.

                    NAUGHT
          That's how easy it will be.

He tosses the glass into the overhead darkness.
When it doesn't fall, MURMURS arise from the
students.

                    NAUGHT
          A miracle? No. My assistant caught
          the glass. We will be moving beyond
          the realm of trickery and deception.

                    STUDENT #1
          When do we get paid?

                    NAUGHT
               (tolerant smile)
          Weekly increments. You must learn to
          have patience when dealing with the
          government, and the paranormal. I've
          selected you out of thousands of
          applicants. You each exhibit promise.
          And your ambitions will be rewarded
          with... yes, illumination.

                    STUDENT #2
          You said it will be easy. What are
          the risks?

                    NAUGHT
In a world without risk, Mr. Dover,
you'd never strive to be president.
Nor would you have volunteered to
participate in this research.
          (points)
You want to make contact with your
dead sister. To make amends. But she
already forgives you. You were nine.
It was an accident. Not your fault.

                    STUDENT #2
How could you possibly -

                    NAUGHT
Accept that I do. We are force fields
of biochemical energy. We have hidden
portals of uncharted knowledge. What
I'm offering you all will enhance who
you already are. It is, after all,
your mind.

TITLE: NINE YEARS LATER

INT. CIA WEAPONS LAB, HIGH SECURITY - Z-DIVISION

Agent DOVER, 33, authoritative, stands next to
OSAKI, 40.

NAUGHT, 54, nods to his male ASSISTANT, 25, who
unscrews a pool cue used for playing billiards.
A cylindrical device (same object seen in Cori's
hand) slides out from the hollow shaft.

                    NAUGHT
     A flawless fit.

                    DOVER
It's fail-safe?

                    NAUGHT
Given the content? Human handlers?

                    DOVER
Some assurance.

                    NAUGHT
There's a rumor your aim is for a
senate seat. Where to next?

                    OSAKI
Assurance this will work.

Naught moves to a white board, picks up a marker.

                    NAUGHT
Let's do this old school.
          (writes)
PICKARD: EVIL. STIKES: BAD -

                    DOVER
Stikes is a bad agent.

                    NAUGHT
But not a traitor. He's convincing.
And Cori, as infiltrator, is the
connecting tissue that pulls this
plan together to work. I repeat -

HE UNDERLINES: "PICKARD: EVIL. STIKES: BAD.
CORI: GOOD."

                    OSAKI
Don't be an ass.

                    NAUGHT
          (ignores him)
Once Cori returns stateside, she
reconnects to surprise Stikes and
initiate a love relationship.

                    OSAKI
That simple.

                    NAUGHT
Have you seen my daughter?

NAUGHT (cont'd)
(at Dover)
Next, she communicates to Pickard,
who she's been working for, of a top
secret pathogen I've developed.

DOVER
To be used how? As a weapon?

NAUGHT
It's an aggressive respiratory virus
that is rapidly transmittable, and
deadly. Released globally, it would
cause a pandemic and nations to fail.
Pickard wants to create this chaos.

DOVER
How do you know that?

NAUGHT
Accept that I do.

OSAKI
He'd put his own life at risk.

NAUGHT
He believes he's invulnerable.
(at Dover)
Back to our chain of events. Cori
informs Pickard that Stikes has
stolen one of these devices and is
willing to sell it, but only to
Pickard if done in person.

OSAKI
He'd never come.

NAUGHT
He will. It's personal.

OSAKI
Meaning?

NAUGHT
They share a history.

OSAKI
He'll suspect it's a trap.

NAUGHT
He will come because Pickard trusts
Cori. The location will be pre-
arranged. When the trade is made,
you'll have conclusive proof of his
culpability and criminality. And
you'll have captured your nemesis.

OSAKI
Too damned risky. If this toxin -

NAUGHT
Agent Osaki, when the enemy has no
nation, has no ideology other than
annihilation. It sends a very clear
message. The Age of Debate is over.
And drastic measures are required.

DOVER
Chemical weapons have been outlawed
by the CWC. What would happen, let's
say, if this virus got released?

NAUGHT
Airborne chemicals are analogous to
missiles coursing through the inner
space we call us. With a calculated
guess, but never a certainty, as to
what doors they will unlock.

DOVER
Damn it, Naught. Assurance we won't
be responsible for Armageddon.

NAUGHT
Gentlemen, in God we must trust.

> OSAKI

Fuck that. How will Pickard know if
this damned thing is even real?

Naught's assistant touches the cylinder with a
pocket scanner.

An LCD reading displays a chemical analysis.

> NAUGHT

He will have a similar scanner for
verification of the viral antigens.

Dover takes possession of the cylinder. He hands
the cue sticks to Osaki. At Naught, Dover
gestures toward an office.

INT. NAUGHT'S OFFICE, CIA WEAPONS LAB - SAME

Dover, alone with Naught, turns on him as the
door shuts.

> DOVER

I asked for a decoy. Not a weapon!

> NAUGHT

The contents are hermetically sealed
in a titanium armature. The timing
mechanism triggers a signal, but will
not release the pathogen.

> DOVER

A false positive.

> NAUGHT

Exquisite bait to catch our prey.

> DOVER

You must be proud of yourself for
creating a monster. Who has now
become an international terrorist and
mass murderer.

                    NAUGHT
Pickard, as he calls himself now, is
not my creation. I can't control his
actions. Nor is there concrete proof
yet of his liability. You need this.

                    DOVER
Have you been enjoying incarceration?

                    NAUGHT
Oh, yes, I'm a dedicated servant.

                    DOVER
You destroyed government property.

                    NAUGHT
Tragic. It was <u>mine</u> to destroy.

Dover picks up a framed photo off Naught's desk.

CLOSE ON image of a younger man, Naught, with
his wife and two children.

                    DOVER
I want Pickard dead or in a cage.

                    NAUGHT
As do I.

                    DOVER
Happier times, or more pretense?

                    NAUGHT
At heart, I am still a family man.

                    DOVER
You murdered your wife.

                    NAUGHT
Untrue. And I was exonerated.

Dover PLOPS the frame onto papers cluttering the desk.

NAUGHT
My daughter loves me.

DOVER
Is she programed to say that?

Naught, annoyed, gives Dover a contrite smile.

NAUGHT
Cori has an exemplary mind.

DOVER
You raised your kids like lab rats.
What you did was reprehensible.

Naught calmly uprights the framed family photo.

Dover holds up the cylindrical device between
their eyes.

DOVER
There's no room for errors here.

NAUGHT
Cori is a needed asset. Admit it.

DOVER
She'd better be working for us.

NAUGHT
We call it covert for a reason.

DOVER
(head shake)
You even had her killed too.

NAUGHT
And then brought her back to life.
Cori possesses extraordinary gifts.

DOVER
So did Pandora.

Dover opens the door to leave. He stops, looks back.

> DOVER
> The mind can only take so much.

> NAUGHT
> Mr. Dover, the mind has no limits.

> DOVER
> Maybe it should.

INT. CIA WEAPONS LAB, Z-DIVISION - MOMENTS LATER

Naught and his assistant escort Dover and Osaki to doors where military officers are stationed on the other side.

> DOVER
> Worst case scenario, hypothetically, if these contents went airborne?

> NAUGHT
> A catalyst for everlasting peace.
> I jest. Good day, gentlemen.

A guard unlocks the door. The two agents exit and the door closes and locks behind them. Naught rubs his eyes.

> NAUGHT
> Lord, what fools these mortals be.

> ASSISTANT
> Sir?

> NAUGHT
> Shakespeare. Try guessing this one:
> Some think it is peace I have come to cast upon the world. They do not know it is really dissension.

His assistant, used to these mind games, shakes his head.

                    NAUGHT
      Jesus of Nazareth, my dear boy.

INT. CRAZY EIGHT BAR, BERKELEY - NIGHT

Cori Videri, at 27, is the essence of bohemian
beauty. Seated at the bar, she stands and moves
to watch something.

ROBERT STIKES, 29, is playing billiards. He is a
confident man, aware of his good looks. After a
shot he holds the cue stick behind his neck,
wrists over the ends, relaxed, waiting his turn.
His next shot sinks two balls in opposite
pockets with the cue ball bouncing off the table
cushion and striking the 8-ball, sinking it
last. He acts surprised by his luck and win.

Cori, leaning against a wall, is watching. He
sees her and walks toward her. His curious grin
turns to stupefaction.

                    STIKES
      No way. You can't be real.

                    CORI
      I can even walk and talk too.

                    STIKES
      I'm Robert.

                    CORI
      Cori Videri.

                    STIKES
      The hell you are.

                    CORI
      Surprise.

INT. CRAZY EIGHT BAR, BERKELEY - LATER

Cori and Stikes sit at a table sipping beers,

assessing each other. He sniffs the air and looks at her chest.

CLOSE ON HER T-SHIRT THAT SAYS "ARTISTIC LICENSE."

                    STIKES
          Turpentine. You still paint. And your
          breasts have developed nicely.

                    CORI
          I moved here last month. I've been
          living on an island off of Greece.
          I'm taking night classes. And these,
          they're not really mine.

                    STIKES
               (laughs)
          Then whose are they?

                    CORI
          Technically my father owns them since
          he paid for the upgrade.

                    STIKES
          I can't believe you're alive.

                    CORI
          I can't believe you care.

                    STIKES
          Cori, you died. I witnessed it.

                    CORI
          My death was highly overrated.

                    STIKES
          Staged?

                    CORI
          No, I died.

                    STIKES
          Then clarify what the fuck happened.

                    CORI
You mean did I see a toilet flush of
glorious light and angels? No.

                    STIKES
I attended your fucking funeral.

                    CORI
Okay, now that was staged.

                    STIKES
I'll never forgive your father for
what he did to us. Especially you.

                    CORI
Did you know that the male praying
mantis can't copulate with its head
attached to its body. So the female
bites it off before they have sex.

                    STIKES
          (laughs)
Message received. I'll stop.

                    CORI
My turn. What happened to you?

                    STIKES
I'm still alive. I freelance, repair
computers, tech support, whatever.

                    CORI
No. You're a pool hustler.

                    STIKES
That's only for fun.

                    CORI
That's sad. Pissing away your gift.

                    STIKES
It's not so bad. Are you that good?

> CORI
Not really. I'm trying to be.

> ROBERT
Then I admire you for trying.

> CORI
> (dismissive)
You can turn off the charm. I'm not
about to get involved with you.

> ROBERT
For a second there, it almost felt
like we were already involved.

TITLE: THREE MONTHS LATER

INT. CRAZY EIGHT BAR - ANOTHER NIGHT

At a nearby table, Cori sketches on a pad while
Stikes plays billiards with two men, PICKARD and
MARTINO.

The SKETCH is of Stikes. A fly lands on his face.

A SWIPE of her hand catches the fly, its wings
held between her finger and thumb.

> CORI
You want to die? Get lost.

She FLICKS away the fly. She is then startled by -

AN ANGEL, A TRANSPARENT WOMAN, WHO IS STARING AT
HER FROM ACROSS THE ROOM.

Pickard hands Stikes a wad of money then departs
out a side door with Martino.

Stikes sits beside Cori and slips the money into
her purse. He sets his pool cue next to another
one leaning against the table.

                    STIKES
That was fun, beating Pickard. And
now, predictably, he wants a rematch.

                    CORI
You enjoy this too much.

                    STIKES
I can't believe you've actually been
working for that prick.

                    CORI
Worked. As in past tense.

                    STIKES
          (inhales)
Time to make a deal with the devil.

Stikes grabs for the other pool cue and Cori
grabs his arm, stopping him.

                    CORI
I changed my mind. Let's leave.

                    STIKES
Leave? And then what?

                    CORI
Disappear. Go anywhere.

Stikes squints and leans in for a fast kiss but
Cori holds him tight in a passionate, desperate
embrace. He breaks free and jokes -

                    STIKES
Wow. The ice caps are melting. This
global warming I like. But stay cool,
all right, until this transaction is
made. After that we can go anywhere
you want.

                    CORI
Don't do it, Rob. I'm serious.

Stikes unscrews the pool cue and surreptitiously slides the device out and hands it to Cori.

> STIKES
> I don't trust him either. For safe keeping. I'll make sure the prick has the rest of the money first.

INT. CRAZY EIGHT BAR, REST ROOM - MOMENTS LATER

The faucet water flows with BLOOD. Cori looks up and is STARTLED by a ghost in the mirror. It's Stikes with his face slashed and throat cut.

EXT./INT. SERIES OF SHOTS - NIGHT

A) A derelict FIRES an automatic weapon into a parked car.

B) At an open hotel window, from inside the room, a sniper is SHOT from behind.

C) Inside a surveillance van with monitoring equipment, Dover and Osaki begin to SHOUT.

EXT. ALLEY, BEHIND CRAZY EIGHT BAR - SAME

Cori BURSTS into an alley through a back door of the bar.

Stikes is cornered against a wall. Pickard holds a knife. Martino holds the unscrewed pool cue and tosses both pieces at Stikes.

> STIKES
> Cori, run!

Stikes' face is CUT with a knife, then his throat.

Cori, in shock, staggers backward, and runs into the street.

> FLASHBACK TO:

21

INT. LECTURE ROOM - NIGHT

Same twelve college students are observing
Professor Naught.

CLOSE ON his eyes twitching minutely.

> NAUGHT
> Time is made of discrete particles.
> Each brain will processes this
> genetic enhancement differently.

CUT TO: Billiard balls BREAKING by a cue ball.

> NAUGHT (V.O.)
> Strive to govern these tiny planets.

INT. CHURCH, A FUNERAL - DAY

The eleven male students and Naught move past an
open casket. Cori, lying inside, is beautiful
even in death.

> BACK TO PRESENT

EXT. UNIVERSITY STREET, BERKELEY - NIGHT

As she runs into the street, Cori is STRUCK down
by a Fiat convertible. Her head strikes the
pavement hard.

INSERT - The sound of BREAKING billiard balls.

Cori regains consciousness. The driver gets out
to help her.

Cori rises, shoves her aside, hijacks the car,
and drives off.

EXT. BAY BRIDGE, OAKLAND/SAN FRANCISCO - NIGHT

A trailer is parked under the bridge beside the bay.

INT. CIA TRAILER, BAY BRIDGE - SAME NIGHT

Four agents are in this crowded space: DOVER is
furious and pacing; RAMOS, 23, grabs a handful
of darts; BRIGGS, 25, rubs her bandaged thigh;
OSAKI is holding a cell phone.

              OSAKI
Roger that. Seven agents! All dead!

              BRIGGS
We lost Videri.

              RAMOS
Great. Pandora is out of her box.

              BRIGGS
Pandora was the woman not the f-ing
contents - you moron.

              RAMOS
Fuck that. It's a toxic screwup!

              OSAKI
How did Pickard blindside us?

              DOVER
I underestimated his abilities.

The other agents look to him for clarification.

              DOVER
Operation Sandstorm. Like that.

              OSAKI
Like what? We were attached. You had
a premonition there were incoming
missiles even before radar detection.
Which saved our asses. You mean -

              DOVER
That kind of ability. Yes.

                    RAMOS
     Terrific, so now that asshole has a
     chemical pathogen to detonate.

Dover glowers at Ramos who hurls a dart at a
target board. He then turns to Briggs talking on
a cell phone.

                    BRIGGS
     Airports are on alert.

                    DOVER
     But no road blocks. We need Pickard
     to stay surfaced and not burrow.

                    RAMOS
     He's not a bloody mole.

                    DOVER
     Pickard doesn't have the device.

                    OSAKI
     Then who? Videri? Are you certain?

                    RAMOS
     Like you were so certain about -

With alarming speed Dover catches his tossed
dart in midair, grabs Ramos by the throat, and
SHOVES him against the wall.

                    DOVER
     I see more than you can imagine.
     Coordinate with the news stations.
     We need their choppers so we appear
     non-military. Is that understood?

Dover releases his grip on Ramos who rubs his neck.

                    RAMOS
     And tell the reporters what? They'll
     rip us apart like vultures?

                    BRIGGS
     Stolen data. They'll buy that.

                    OSAKI
     Why did they incinerate Stikes?

SCREEN ON MOBILE DEVICE SHOWS A CHARRED BODY IN
THE ALLEY.
                    RAMOS
     I'm gonna obliterate that fuck.

                    DOVER
     We need Pickard alive. Briggs, are
     you up for this?

Briggs lifts her windbreaker to show a bandaged
midriff but no blood.

                    BRIGGS
     Minor penetration. I'm still good.

EXT. STREET, BERKELEY - NIGHT (FLASHBACK)

INSERT - AUTOMATIC WEAPON FIRED INTO A PARKED CAR.

                    RAMOS (V.O.)
     What compelled you to wear a vest?

INT. CIA TRAILER, BAY BRIDGE - SAME

                    BRIGGS
     Excuse me for not dying.

She indicates a bandaged head wound with blood.
Ramos MUTTERS as he exits the trailer. Briggs
follows him. Osaki lingers.

                    DOVER
     I need you in Reno. Take Ramos.

                    OSAKI
     Why Nevada?

                    DOVER
A hunch. We can make this work.

                    OSAKI
Metaphorically?

                    DOVER
        (snaps back)
The cleanup?

                    OSAKI
Smoke and mirrors. Never happened.

                    DOVER
It happened! This is on me. What?

                    OSAKI
Briggs. Being the only survivor.

                    DOVER
What are you implying?

                    OSAKI
Nothing. Like a miracle, is all.

Pondering this, Dover fingers the point of the
dart in his hand. Osaki exits. Dover winces as
the door SLAMS shut.

EXT. HIGHWAY, SIERRA MOUNTAINS - NIGHT (PRESENT)

CUT TO: The mountain cafe receding inside a
rearview mirror.

Through the windshield, Cori observes lights far
below, then -

CLOSE ON a transparent man, a ghost, seated
beside her.

Startled, she hits the brakes. The car SKIDS,
spinning to a stop. The engine dies. The ghost
is gone. She POUNDS the steering wheel.

                    CORI
     Shit!

The engine won't start. APPARITIONS appear in
the road.

                    CORI
     Shit.

The RUMBLING vibrations from a semi-truck coming
toward her from behind is heard.

                    CORI
     Shit!

The truck ROARS past narrowly missing her. She
hugs the steering wheel and CRIES.

EXT. FIAT CONVERTIBLE, SOUTH LAKE TAHOE - NIGHT

Cori is stopped in traffic. A truck filled with
LAUGHING men, who appear drunk, HOWL for her
attention. She ignores them.

EXT. FIAT CONVERTIBLE, SOUTH LAKE TAHOE - SAME

Cori's eyes begin to twitch rapidly. She SLAPS
her face.

                    CORI
     God-damned bugs.

A HORN from behind gets her to acknowledge the
GREEN light.

She accelerates then brakes, almost hitting a
man in the crosswalk. His head turns. It's
Professor NAUGHT. He fades away.

EXT. FIAT CONVERTIBLE, SOUTH LAKE TAHOE - LATER

Cori comes to a stop at a RED light. She shuts
her eyes.

> A VOICE (O.C.)
> Hey, Babe, what's the problem. Do you
> need a place to stay tonight?

Inside another convertible is a man who smiles.
His face MORPHS into a vision of evil before
returning to a smile.

> CORI
> Thanks. I'm fine.

CUT TO: BRIGHT LIGHTS OF TOWERING CASINOS UP
AHEAD IN THE DISTANCE.

> CORI (V.O.)
> It's one big lie, isn't it? Like
> shimmering lakes seen on a desert.
> Fortunes found in a cookie. Lucky
> numbers scribbled on a toilet wall.

EXT. FIAT, CASINO PARKING LOT - LATE NIGHT

Cori opens the glove box, finding sunglasses and
a baseball cap. She ties her hair into a
ponytail and puts on the cap. She searches her
purse, removes the cylindrical device and
examines it with a puzzled expression, before
hiding it beneath the seat. While massaging the
back of her head and staring in the rearview
mirror, she asks -

> CORI
> Why are we here? Think.

EXT. CASINO PARKING LOT - SAME

Cori is crouched behind the car unscrewing and
swapping license plates.

INT. REGISTRATION DESK, CASINO HOTEL LOBBY - NIGHT

She passes through security. She notices a sign.

INSERT - GLOBAL ONE INTERNATIONAL SUMMIT CONFERENCE

Cori avoids looking at security cameras on the ceiling as she smiles at the CLERK at the hotel registration desk.

> CLERK
> Do you have a reservation?

> CORI
> Yes, I believe I do.

Cori searches her purse and pulls out a credit card.

> CLERK
> And the name?

> CORI
> Nolan. Corina.

INT. BATHROOM, CASINO HOTEL - LATER

Cori is reclined in a bathtub. Exhausted, her eyelids close.

INSERT - STIKES' THROAT SLASHED BY PICKARD'S KNIFE

Cori SPLASHS bath water as she's STARTLED awake. She stands and reaches for a towel. There is a persistant KNOCKING.

> CORI
> Just a minute!

INT. HALLWAY, CASINO HOTEL - LATER

Through the peephole, Cori views a vacant hallway.

INT. HOTEL, CASINO HOTEL - LATER

Wrapped in a towel, Cori sits on the bed. She lays back, her eyes closed. She looks up and quickly covers herself.

CUT TO: Cori looking back at herself in a
mirrored ceiling.

INT. BATHROOM, CASINO HOTEL - LATER

Cori inspects the side of her head and the
noticeable lump. She puts the hat back on,
stares at herself, TAPS the glass.

                    CORI
          Why am I here? Focus.

INT. ELEVATOR, CASINO HOTEL - LATER

Mirrored walls show multiple images of Cori. She
looks at her wrist watch and sees the LCD time:
3:33. It sparks a memory.

                    CORI
          Three threes. This mean something.
          Jackpot numbers maybe. Lucky me.

INT. MAIN FLOOR, CASINO HOTEL - EARLY MORNING

NOISE of roulette wheels SPINNING. Slot machines
VOMIT coins. Men MURMURING as their eyes express
a desire to devour her.

                    CORI (V.O.)
          Pleasure Island. Where boys turn into
          mules and the girls turn tricks.

INT. MAIN FLOOR, CASINO HOTEL - LATER

Past the blackjack tables, an ANGEL is staring
at Cori from across the room. It is the same
transparent woman she had seen at the cafe.

Cori looks away and inserts a dollar into the
nearest slot machine.

The wheels STOP on gold bars. It triggers HORNS
and BELLS!

                    CORI
     Shit!

She glances at the ceiling before walking fast
for the doors.

                    GAMBLER (O.C.)
          Hey! Come back! You won!

EXT. FIAT CONVERTIBLE, MOUNTAIN HWY, NEVADA - DAWN

Cori BANGS the steering wheel with her fist. She
is driving, hunched and shivering. The sky is
overcast.

                    CORI
          A god-damn jackpot! And I run away.
               (looks up)
          You must be enjoying this.

EXT. FIAT, MOUNTAIN HWY, NEVADA - LATER

Cori slows to the side of a deserted two-lane
road to look at a piece of paper she has in her
hand with directions.

                    CORI
          Jesus. Where in hell do you live?

She U-turns and crosses the highway. Set back
from the road is an ornate cross, like a grave
marker forged out of iron.

EXT. FIAT CONVERTIBLE, DIRT ROAD - SAME

The convertible PUTTERS along like a motorboat.

She sees a man in the woods then realizes its a
sculpture. The road turns and she SCREAMS, then
CURSES the metal python hanging over the road
from the limb of a tree.

EXT. A WOODED AREA, OFF DIRT ROAD - SAME

Cori buries the stash of money under rocks next
to a girl sculpted from metal junk, a NYMPH
blowing into a long flute (a golf club). Cori
sits on a rock and stares at the girl.

                    CORI
          Look at us. Freaks of nature.

Cori removes the cylindrical device from her purse.

                    CORI
          Robert died because of you.

The nymph's ball-bearing eyes depict innocence.

                    CORI
          God damn you, Robert!

Cori stand and KICKS - dislodging the nine-iron
flute in the nymph's hands. She kneels and lifts
up the girl's metal foot, a cooking pot, and
hides the cylindrical device beneath it.

EXT. FIAT CONVERTIBLE, DIRT ROAD - LATER

Cori gives the metal snake her middle finger and
drives on. She passes a sign, HUNK OF JUNK.
There are more sculptures — a serpent, a miner
panning for gold, a gargoyle in a tree.

                    CORI (V.O.)
          Where have I landed?

A wasteland of junk passes on both sides, mostly
CARS. The road opens to a driveway that circles
a fountain. Behind it is a two-story stucco
house. To the left is a garden and a sculpture
of NEPTUNE holding a TRIDENT. A colonnade
extends downhill toward a POND with a tiny
ISLAND. To the house's right is a corrugated
BARN painted in a wash of colors.

Cori parks, gets out, HONKS the horn. KYLE
GARRETT, 33, a man with long hair and a beard,
exits the barn. They walk toward each other. Light
breaks through the clouds and shines upon Cori who
resembles a wayward angel having fallen to Earth.

                    GARRETT
I must be hallucinating. You're the
most beautiful sight I've ever seen.

                    CORI
Are you Kyle?

                    GARRETT
That's right. Call me KG.

                    CORI
Cagey?

                    GARRETT
Kyle Austin Garrett. K.A.G. And you -
you have to be Cori.

                    CORI
How did you know?

                    GARRETT
Rob. He's mentioned you.

                    CORI
Robert's dead. He was murdered.

Garrett closes his eyes, pained by the news.

                    GARRETT
    How?

An awkward silence ensues as he studies her.

                    CORI
What? Don't look at me like that. I
loved him. I had nothing to do with
it. I mean - Jesus! Forget I came.

She turns to leave. An apparition is seated in her car.

> GARRETT
> I never accused you.

> CORI
> He was knifed after a billiards game. I don't know by who or why!

> GARRETT
> Okay, I believe you. Calm down. Are you in some kind of trouble?

> CORI
> I don't know. No. I wasn't sure where to go. Robert said I should come here if anything bad happened.

> GARRETT
> You're welcome to stay. It's just -

> CORI
> What?

> GARRETT
> You. Suddenly showing up, looking like this lost angel. And informing me that Robert was murdered.
> (pulls at his beard)
> Cori, I appreciate you telling me. It's just - you're projecting some very strange vibes.

> CORI
> Vibes? What are you, some hippie who lives off the land, is that it?

> GARRETT
> (amused)
> Would you like some breakfast?

INT. GARRETT'S ART STUDIO - MORNING

He looks directly at Cori as they sit at a
kitchen nook.

                    GARRETT
          Excuse me for staring. Bad habit.

                    CORI
          Help yourself.

She pretends not to care and shakes Cheerios
from a box into a bowl. She views the vast room
with its sculptures, forge, acetylene tanks,
canvases. She pours milk from a pitcher.

                    CORI
          From the cow's utter this morning?

                    GARRETT
          Civilization starts inside the mind,
          not at the corner market. It's a
          short drive from here. Anything else
          you'd like to know?

                    CORI
          That was rude. Sorry. I didn't expect
          my life to get this bad.

                    GARRETT
          Nor did I expect to see you.
              (sad smile)
          Can you tell me what happened?

                    CORI
          Oh, right. I'm not sure, exactly. It
          was horrible. I told the police what
          I knew. Which wasn't much. I'd rather
          not talk about it right now.

She sees a scar across his broken nose. It
extends over his mouth into his bearded jaw. She
looks away at his artwork.

                    CORI
        You've been busy. These all yours?

                    GARRETT
        Until I set them free. They sorta
        haunt the grounds.

                    CORI
        I've noticed.

                    GARRETT
        It's nicer when you smile.

She shivers and yawns. He stands, meanders over
to a work area. As he prepares to ignite a
welder's torch, he says -

                    GARRETT
        About Rob. Why don't we talk when you
        feel ready. I keep an open house.
        Find a room and settle in. It's
        peaceful here. You look as though you
        could use some sleep.

EXT. PORTICO, GARRETT'S HOUSE - MORNING

Cori stops to admire a large sculpture - a naked
woman lying on her side. She touches the front
door. It CREAKS open.

INT. LIVING ROOM, GARRETT'S HOUSE - SAME

Cori sees murals of gigantic gods and goddesses.
They are magnificently executed and strange. The
walls are curved with openings. A walkway leads
to the second floor.

INT. SECOND FLOOR BEDROOM, GARRETT'S HOUSE - SAME

Cori drops her purse. Sun shines in from a
window which she shutters off. She lies down on
the bed and closes her eyes.

INT. BEDROOM, GARRETT'S HOUSE - NIGHT

Darkness. Then a hand on a light switch. Cori
clutches a quilted blanket. She lets it drop and
lifts her sweater.

She examines her naked chest in a mirror and
glances with suspicion at the unlocked bedroom
door. Her fingers trace the minute scar lines
from surgery beneath her breasts.

INT. SECOND FLOOR RAILING, GARRETT'S HOUSE - NIGHT

Cori sees Garrett reading in an armchair. He
looks up.

                    GARRETT
          Coals are heating outside. I hope
          you're hungry.

                    CORI
          What time is it?

EXT. GARDEN, GARRETT'S PROPERTY - NIGHT

Cori and Garrett sit beside a glowing barbecue pit.

                    CORI
          I was more tired than I thought.
          I guess you provided the blanket?

He nods and removes patties and corn cobs from a
cooler. Cori crosses her arms. She brings her
knees together.

                    GARRETT
          Sleep is underrated as a need.

He removes a plastic pitcher from the cooler.

                    GARRETT
          Care for a cocktail?

                    CORI
          I don't drink alcohol.

                    GARRETT
          It's Kool-Aid. Lemon-Lime.

                    CORI
          Or take drugs.

                    GARRETT
          I too prefer a clear mind.

                    CORI
          How do I know it's not laced with
          LSD, or some date-rape barbiturate?

                    GARRETT
          You're not very trusting, are you?

                    CORI
          No.

EXT. GARDEN, GARRETT'S PROPERTY - SAME

Cori gazes into the coals, wincing as she sips
her drink.

                    GARRETT
          Care to talk about it?

                    CORI
          What? Oh, right. These men must have
          known Rob was cheating them.

                    GARRETT
          I told him he should quit that.

                    CORI
          He'd won nine hundred dollars.

                    GARRETT
          What a waste. You were there?

                    CORI
          No. I left early.

He shakes his head. The patties SIZZLE on the grill.

                    GARRETT
          I knew about the hustling, but, some-
          thing doesn't feel right.

                    CORI
          The world's not right. Have you been
          out to see it lately?

                    GARRETT
          Not lately.

                    CORI
          Kids are carrying guns to school. A
          woman got shot in the head as she
          watched TV. Bullet went through her
          wall — bang, the end. The world's a
          mess. What do you expect?

                    GARRETT
          I expect more. How are you holding
          up? Are you all right?

                    CORI
          I wouldn't know what 'all right' is.

The SILENCE is ruptured by a CROAKING noise.

                    CORI
          What is that?

                    GARRETT
          Bullfrogs. Down at the pond.

                    CORI
          They're loud.

                    GARRETT
          You should hear them when they mate.

His smile is playful. She tenses, looks away, then back.

                    CORI
          You keep staring at me like you're
          expecting something. Don't.

Garrett's hand slowly reaches toward her chest.

                    GARRETT
          Hold still.

Cori swiftly grabs and torques his wrist, forcing Garrett to the ground. She stands, her foot pressed on his neck.

Garrett, at her mercy, stares up at her.

                    CORI
          Don't ever try to touch me.

                    GARRETT
          Okay, I'll let you get the spider.

Cori sees the large insect crawling up her sweater.

                    CORI
          Shit - Shit!

She SWATS and knocks the spider to the ground. Her foot CRUSHES it.

Garrett gets up, reseats himself, rubs his wrist, and stares.

                    GARRETT
          That was more than interesting.

                    CORI
          I'm sorry. I thought. I'm sorry.

She sits, embarrassed. Her vulnerability confuses him.

                    GARRETT
     Let's clear the air, shall we.
     You show up and tell me Robert's
     dead, and that you loved him. So I'll
     trust you on that. Also, I'm
     expecting nothing in return for my
     hospitality. Except a smile, maybe an
     ounce of gratitude, and people
     telling me the truth, if they can.

                    CORI
     What's that supposed to mean?

                    GARRETT
     I am fond of women, yes.

Garrett scoops up a cooked pattie with a spatula
and sets it on one half of a hamburger bun and
hands her the plate.

                    GARRETT
     But lately I like being left alone.
     Here's your cheeseburger. Let's hope
     it's done to your satisfaction.

                                   FADE TO BLACK
INT. CORI'S BEDROOM - NIGHT

Cori SCREAMS in her sleep. She wakes disoriented.

INT. CORI'S BEDROOM - MORNING

Cori, in bed, listens as Garrett moves about
downstairs.

INT. FOYER, GARRETT'S HOUSE - MORNING

Cori finds a note push-pinned to the kitchen
door.

NOTE: I AM IN THE STUDIO WORKING. MAKE YOURSELF
AT HOME.

She decides to snoop around. Each room is
decorated with elaborate ironwork and murals.
She discovers a SAFE behind a painting. It
requires a key to open. She finds no key.

INT. GARRETT'S STUDIO - MORNING

Cori enters through the open door. Garrett CLIPS
the arms of a woman, a sculpture, with metal
shears as if pruning a tree.

                    CORI
          About last night, I'm sorry.

                    GARRETT
          Apology accepted.

                    CORI
          Who's that?

                    GARRETT
          Daphne. Apollo was smitten by her.
          But she only cared for the hunt.
          She avoided him and feared love.

                    CORI
          And became a tree? Real smart.

                    GARRETT
          Do you know the story?

                    COR1
          No. Where's Apollo?

                    GARRETT
          In here somewhere.

She sees a sculpted head of a man, emerging from
rings of wire, his mouth open, inches from
biting a dangling apple.

                    GARRETT
          Tantalus.

CORI
Excuse me?

GARRETT
He's derived from another myth.

Cori is drawn to a small bronze sculpture - a woman wrapped in a swirling garment as if rising from a thick atmosphere.

CORI
What about her?

GARRETT
She's an enigma. No name yet.

Cori sees an emerald settee upon a drop cloth over the floor. On the wall is a large oil painting depicting an entity with colorful wings rising out from a dark turbulent world.

GARRETT
I prefer the human form. The rest of the world is periphery. Not that it doesn't matter. It does.

CORI
You're very good.

GARRETT
God will be the judge on that. But thanks for saying so.

In the center of a table is a glass sphere. She jokes -

CORI
You have a crystal ball.

GARRETT
Care for a psychic reading?

CORI
(laughs, skeptical)

They sit at the table. He splays his hands upon
the sphere.

                    GARRETT
          Hum, I'm receiving - skepticism.

Cori's frown changes to a smile.

                    GARRETT
          The satellite I transmit from just
          went dead. Shall we try later.

                    CORI
          That's it?

He grabs for a deck of cards and begins shuffling.

                    GARRETT
          The Tarot? Okay, now cut the cards
          however you like. Excellent.

Cori is amused, entertained for the first time
in days.

                    GARRETT
          I had to be immersed in a cauldron of
          boiling oil before receiving the
          secrets behind this ageless wisdom.
          Ha, the maiden scoffs!

He places 10 cards face down, then slowly turns
them over: The Magician, The Fool, Wheel of
Fortune, Justice, The Moon, The Hermit, The
Devil, The Tower, Death, The Lovers.

                    CORI
          What's my prognosis?

                    GARRETT
          They're all from the Major Arcana.

                    CORI
          What does that mean?

                    GARRETT
None of them are Cups, Swords, Rods,
or Pentacles. Not to worry.

                    CORI
I like the looks of that, The Moon.

                    GARRETT
A yearning for fulfillment. Except
the card's upside-down. It tends to
mean peace will follow after perils.

                    CORI
The Devil? Not to worry. How do you
put a positive spin on that one?

                    GARRETT
Can't. A destructive force. Tells of
someone lacking in humanity.

                    CORI
You mean like a sociopath.

                    GARRETT
My interpretation too. You do have
some good within the mix.

                    CORI
Like Death. A nice card to receive.

                    GARRETT
Not always literal. It can mean a
rebirth in consciousness. Or simply a
major change in your life.

                    CORI
Death usually does.

Sunlight suddenly fills the room. She jokes -

                    CORI
Here comes that illumination reboot
you've been waiting for.

                    45

                    GARRETT
You have a good heart. But you've
made bad choices. I see your father
having a bad influence on you.

                    CORI
He's dead.

                    GARRETT
You are on a quest, of a spiritual
kind, but you lack guidance.

Cori taps a finger on The Hermit card.

                    CORI
What about him?

                    GARRETT
There to counsel the seeker.

                    CORI
Is that where you fit in?

                    GARRETT
I never have.
        (squints)
Do you feel as if the Devil is
chasing after you?

                    CORI
What kind of a question is that?

Garret indicates The Devil card.

                    GARRETT
Anything I said remotely ring true?

                    CORI
Not really. The Lovers. Is that
supposed to be us?

                    GARRETT
Maybe in our next life.

Garrett sweeps up the cards.

>   CORI
>   How did you know about my father?

>   GARRETT
>   With all those vibes? I don't need
>   cards to tell me.
>   (smiles)
>   Sorry. I didn't mean to upset you.

>   CORI
>   Yes, you did.

EXT. POOLSIDE, CASINO, LAKE TAHOE - DAY

JAMES PICKARD, 32, is seated at a table beside
the pool. Though handsome, he projects an aura
of mercurial danger that is equally repellent
and appealing.

A cocktail WAITRESS is facing the other way,
taking drink orders. He PRICKS her curvaceous
bottom with his toothpick.

>   WAITRESS
>   Ouch! Hey! What the -

>   PICKARD
>   My glass is empty. I need a refill.

>   WAITRESS
>   Did you just poke me with that?

He hands her fifty dollars.

>   PICKARD
>   Fifty more if you can remember what I
>   was drinking.

Her eyes cool to a playful smile.

                    WAITRESS
        I was busy, but okay. Jack, rocks.

                    PICKARD
        Your powers astound me. Be swift and
        you shall receive your bounty.

She departs and people seated nearby GRUMBLE
complaints.

                    PICKARD
        Did I interrupt the order of things?

Pickard grins and places the toothpick back in
his mouth.

He's busy searching the internet on his mobile
device when the waitress returns. He puts a key
in her miniskirt pocket.

                    PICKARD
        Charge it to my room. 6-6-6.

                    WAITRESS
        We don't have a -

                    PICKARD
        My mistake. 66. Like that route.

She removes the key and sets it on the table.

                    WAITRESS
        You promised me an extra fifty.

                    PICKARD
        Come up to my room at 6 sharp to
        collect it. Stay for a drink and
        there will be an extra hundred.

                    WAITRESS
        I don't... That's not my thing.

PICKARD
I'm willing to make it a thousand.

WAITRESS
Yeah, sure. And I'll bet your thing
is about as big as that toothpick.

He holds his smile as she STOMPS off. He
redirects his eyes on his neighbors, LAUGHING.
He gives a menacing look.

PICKARD
Careless words are costly. Like
gospel. Absolute. Like death.

Their smiles drop. MARTINO walks up with a news
clipping.

MARTINO
They had the damn thing posted on the
toilet wall. Recognize anyone?

PICKARD
I knew she'd show up here.

Martino is smoothing down his combed-over hairs.

PICKARD
Face it, Tino. Your head resembles
the posterior of a pongo pygmaeus.

MARTINO
Huh?

PICKARD
And orangutan's butt.

MARTINO
What's eat'n you?

Pickard removes his toothpick and SNAPS the wood
in two.

                        PICKARD
        Cori. She's malfunctioning.

Martino devours a candy bar and licks his fingers.

                        MARTINO
        Kicked Jake in the balls then runs.
        You think the Feds got to her?

                        PICKARD
        She knows better than to betray me.

                        MARTINO
        I say we punt. Do this later.

                        PICKARD
        No, it happens now. The conference?
        You lack ambition. I forgive you.

                        MARTINO
        Big of you. What about the Feds?

                        PICKARD
        I forgive them too.

                        MARTINO
        Very funny.

                        PICKARD
        I do admire their devotion.
             (sips his whiskey)
        By their rules, we're still innocent
        until proven otherwise.

Pickard attracts the smiles of women in swim suits.

                        MARTINO
        Why'd you set him on fire? Stikes was
        already dead. Some bad history
        between you two, huh?

Pickard opens his hand to reveal a 2-shot
derringer.

> MARTINO
> Jeezz, put that fucker away. This
> isn't the Wild West.

> PICKARD
> I plan to reinvent history.

> MARTINO
> With a deadly pathogen? I don't like
> it. The stakes are too high.

> PICKARD
> Survival of the fittest. A needed
> thinning of the herd. Where only the
> vulnerable die. I predict roughly a
> third of the population.

> MARTINO
> Where the hell's that waitress?

Pickard FLINGS ice cubes in his glass into the pool.

> PICKARD
> God-damn that Cori. We have less than
> a week now to detonate that thing.

> MARTINO
> How do you know this new toxin won't
> kill us off too?

> PICKARD
> My manifesto is self preservation.
> Trust me, we're safe. We're alpha
> males. Protective gear when released.
> An international conference will
> transmit and disperse the virus
> worldwide, causing a global pandemic.

A child in diapers toddles up, offering his
stuffed animal to Martino.

> MARTINO
> Naw, you keep him. For protection.

A nervous woman grabs the boy's hand and backs away.

                    MARTINO
          Cute kid. I had a teddy bear once.

                    PICKARD
          I never was a kid.

INT. MAIN FLOOR, CASINO - NIGHT

Pickard holds cards at a poker table. A RINGTONE
of Wagner's Ride of the Valkyries is heard.

                    PICKARD
          This had better beat a royal flush.

He finds Martino playing BlackJack and SLAPS him
on the back.

                    PICKARD
          Fold, we're leaving now. Don't ask.

EXT. CASINO PARKING LOT - NIGHT

Pickard stands beside a Mercedes. Martino is
seated inside.

                    MARTINO
          I thought we were in a big rush.

                    PICKARD
          Payback.

The cocktail WAITRESS exits a back door.

A hand covers her mouth. A knife is held at her
throat. The knife stays as her hair is grabbed,
forcing her head down.

                    PICKARD (O.C.)
          Convince me you want to suck it.
          Bigger than you thought, isn't it?
          That's right. That's my girl.

Shoved to the cement, she looks up. Her eyes
express alarm.

                    PICKARD (O.C.)
          Keep this between us. Or you die.

She SCREAMS as he stabs his toothpick into her cheek.

EXT. TRUCK, DRIVEWAY, GARRETT'S PROPERTY - DAY

Osaki and Ramos, wearing cowboy hats, exit the
vehicle.

INT. GARRETT'S STUDIO - SAME

Osaki and Ramos enter through the open door.

Garrett is welding a leaf on Daphne. He chokes
the torch.

                    GARRETT
          She's down by the pond.

                    RAMOS
          We know.

                    GARRETT
          Mind telling me what happened?

                    OSAKI
          She didn't tell you?

                    GARRETT
          Something went wrong, obviously.

                    OSAKI
          She stole hyper-sensitive data.

Garrett sighs, gives his visitors a smoldering
stare.

                    GARRETT
          Wonderful news.

                    OSAKI
I see you've made progress.
     (at Daphne)
The story of forbidden love.

                    GARRETT
Unattainable, is more like it.

                    OSAKI
Often synonymous.
     (at Ramos)
Apollo was cursed with a malady no
remedy could cure. Daphne. She was
poison. Forbidden love.

                    RAMOS
Like I give a shit.

                    GARRETT
What is it you want from me?

                    RAMOS
Cooperation.

                    GARRETT
Specifically?

                    OSAKI
Surveillance on your property.

                    RAMOS
We'll need that motor home in your
junkyard. Our vehicles stationed
roadside. We watch and we listen.

                    GARRETT
Listen how?

                    OSAKI
Wire your house and studio.

                    GARRETT
Absolutely not.

                    RAMOS
Are you hiding something?

                    GARRETT
No more than you.

EXT. GARDEN, GARRETT'S PROPERTY - LATER

Garrett, Ramos and Osaki stand at the garden's
edge looking down on Cori in a hammock reading
by the pond. Beside the three men talking at the
top of this gradual slope stands an imposing
bronze-patinated sculpture of Neptune holding
his trident. Osaki unhooks a mobile device from
his belt.

                    OSAKI
No inside bugs. Stations set along
the perimeter. We're in agreement?

                    GARRETT
Tomorrow I'll be going into town.

                    RAMOS
Make sure she goes with you.

Osaki programs a message and sends it.

                    GARRETT
I appreciate the cause, but not the
collateral damage you've caused from
bad judgement.

                    RAMOS
She fouled the plan, not us.

                    GARRETT
You're not telling me everything.
Not that I'd expect it.

                    OSAKI
She brought this on herself.

                    GARRETT
Why don't you just confront her and
ask if she has what you're after.

                    RAMOS
You're missing the point.

                    GARRETT
That being?

                    RAMOS
She's poison.

                    OSAKI
She double-crossed Stikes. She
tricked him and stole the data.

                    RAMOS
She's the kind who'll kill you in
your sleep. You used to have balls,
Garrett. Get with the program.

                    OSAKI
Her car is stolen. She stopped at a
casino. Won a jackpot. A big one.

                    RAMOS
Didn't stay to collect. She ran.

                    OSAKI
But failed to avoid the cameras.

Garrett scratches his beard and chin.

                    GARRETT
How do you propose I explain your
presence here? She'll ask.

                    RAMOS
You're a smart guy, Garrett. Lie.
We're here to look over your junk.

EXT. POND WITH ISLAND, GARRETT'S PROPERTY - SAME

Cori, in a hammock, looks up and notices Garrett
by the house talking with men, Osaki and Ramos,
both wearing cowboy hats.

> CORI (V.O.)
> This filly, boys, ain't for sale.

She pretends to ignore them and returns to the
book. It shows a marble sculpture of Apollo in
pursuit of Daphne, his hand touching her naked
thigh, her mouth expressing shock close to
pleasure. She reads aloud -

> CORI (V.O.)
> He saw her eyes bright as stars, then
> her lips and was not satisfied with
> only seeing them.

She pauses to look up. The men are gone. She
reads on -

> CORI (V.O.)
> A stiffness seized her limbs. He
> embraced and lavished kisses upon
> her. Since you cannot be my wife you
> shall be my very own tree.

INT. KITCHEN, GARRETT'S HOUSE - NIGHT

Cori sets the table while Garrett drains boiled
potatoes.

> CORI
> Daphne. Fable of the laurel tree.
> I stole one of your art books.

> GARRETT
> She was also Apollo's first love.

> CORI
> I guess he had bad luck with women.

                    GARRETT
    Not all. Cupid got mad at Apollo for
    saying little boys shouldn't play
    with weapons. So Cupid shoots Apollo
    through the heart.

                    CORI
    With a golden arrow. And shoots her
    with a shitty one. I didn't know
    Cupid was such a little prick.

                    GARRETT
    Mashed potatoes, okay?

She teases him with a disappointed pout.

                    CORI
    Meat and potatoes, again? Cooking, I
    see, is not your forté. I'll buy
    ingredients tomorrow and surprise you
    with a meal. By the way, those men
    today, who were they?

                    GARRETT
    Customers.

                    CORI
    What exactly did they want?

                    GARRETT
    A door off a '67 Mustang.

                    CORI
    I'm not stupid.

                    GARRETT
    Oh, I know that.

                    CORI
    Were you negotiating some kind of
    trade behind my back?

                    GARRETT
     They thought they'd seen you before.

                     CORI
     And you believed them?

                    GARRETT
     I almost told them we were married.
     But gossip floats around town. So I
     said you were my sister.

                     CORI
     Your sister?

                    GARRETT
     And you weren't the casino type.

                     CORI
     What do you mean?

                    GARRETT
     I had to laugh. They thought you'd be
     someone who'd walk away from a huge
     jackpot. Pretty stupid, huh.

She reacts with confused innocence.

                    GARRETT
     Did you? Walk away from a jackpot?

                     CORI
          Of course not.

INT. GARRETT'S PANEL TRUCK, MT. ROAD - DAY

Garrett and Cori are going downhill. He points
at -

THE DESERT with massive white cumulus clouds,
yellow-rimmed, shadowed in purple, like another
world spanning for miles.

                    GARRETT
        Difficult to capture on paint.
        Moments of divinity such as that.

The truck turns. Through the windshield a street
is seen cresting between pines that leads to a
row of buildings.

                    CORI
        What's the population, about ten?

                    GARRETT
        Let's not get overly optimistic.

EXT. TRUCK AT SIDEWALK, NEVADA TOWN - SAME

They exit and step onto a sidewalk beside a
grocery store.

                    CORI
        I'll be lucky to find half the
        ingredients I'm looking for.

                    GARRETT
        Carson City's a few miles away.
        I need to check my box at the post
        office. I don't mind driving you.

                    CORI
        I'll make do. Where should we meet?

                    GARRETT
        At that cafe. In twenty minutes?

                    CORI
        Sure.

She watches him walk away. His stride is
relaxed. A women springs from a cafe door, grabs
him in a hug. They LAUGH.

EXT. GROCERY STORE, NEVADA TOWN - SAME

Bells CHIME as Cori pushes through the screen door.

INT. GROCERY STORE, NEVADA TOWN - SAME

Cori stands at a pay phone, listening in the
receiver. She presses down the lever. She TAPS
the phone against her head.

> CORI
> Don't be stupid. Think!

INT. RANGE ROVER, NEVADA TOWN - SAME

Briggs watches through the windshield as Dover
crosses the street. He holds styrofoam cups.
She opens the door for him. He slides onto the
driver's seat, hands her a coffee.

> DOVER
> Black. Cream yesterday. You're a hard
> one to pin down, Briggs.

> BRIGGS
> Garrett's at the post office. Videri
> is inside the store.

> DOVER
> You look especially pretty today.

She lifts her arm to brush fingers over his cheek.

> DOVER
> I knew I was in trouble the moment we
> met. You know I love you.

> BRIGGS
> You only think you do.

She looks away, miserable, pretending to watch
the street. Dover sips his coffee and looks over
the cup at her.

                    DOVER
I was approached and asked to run for
Congress next year.

                    BRIGGS
I'd heard the rumors.

                    DOVER
Pickard's killed that option. He's
become my god-damned nemesis.
        (sips coffee)
It's important we stop this. I need a
win. He's tarnished my record.

                    BRIGGS
Shit happens. Even to wonder boys.

                    DOVER
Here she comes.

They watch Cori exit the market and place bags
in the truck.

                    BRIGGS
Why do you trust Garrett?

                    DOVER
I don't. Not completely.

                    BRIGGS
These two could be lovers. Garrett
and Videri. Or her and Pickard?

                    DOVER
I don't see it. But love, I've been
told, can make you blind.
        (cocks head)
I knew her, Videri, years ago.

                    BRIGGS
        (laughs)
Damn you get around.

                    DOVER
Don't get the wrong idea. She's been
a valuable CIA investment. And it's a
good thing she works for us.

                    BRIGGS
Does she?
          (crushes her cup)
I'll see if super girl made a call.
You want anything from inside?

                    DOVER
Candy bar. Chocolate. You decide.

                    BRIGGS
Honk if you need me, Cowboy.

Dover smiles, then watches as Briggs crosses the
street.

INT. GROCERY STORY, NEVADA TOWN - SAME

Briggs silently waits with the pay phone cradled
to her ear.

                    MALE VOICE (V.O.)
Home, Nadine, is a place where you
know love will always be found.

                    BRIGGS
It's not that easy. Is it, Dad?
          (into phone)
Yes. I'm still holding.

                    OPERATOR (V.O.)
You have clearance. The number was
510.562.6321. Shall I connect you?

                    BRIGGS
No, I'll place the call myself.

She keys in numbers. Her anger is brewing.

                    BRIGGS
     Who do you think it is? You lied! I
     was told no one would die. I agreed
     to cooperate because I trusted -

INT. CAFE, NEVADA TOWN - SAME

Cori sips coffee in a window booth and displays
a friendly ease as she talks to a waitress, ERIN
McBRIDE, 45.

                    ERIN
     KG never mentioned a sister. I'd
     offer to traipse you through town
     except you've seen the extent of it.

                    CORI
     It's nice. I like the solitude.

                    ERIN
     That's what keeps me here. I'll make
     the scheduled stops, then come back.

Erin sashays away for comic affect. Cori resumes
her search through a newspaper and stops when
she sees herself.

INSERT - PHOTO WITH HEADLINE:

     "Mystery Woman Flees From Jackpot!"

A RAPPING at the window startles her. She closes
the paper. Garrett holds a box and cocks his
head to say, "Lets go."

INT. GARRETT'S PANEL TRUCK, NEVADA TOWN - SAME

Garrett's eyes narrow on Cori as he opens the
door and sits inside. He SLAPS down an opened
newspaper on the seat.

                    GARRETT
     You want to try some honesty?

She pretends to be puzzled by his words and
lifts the paper.

>   CORI
>   Oh, my God. I see what you mean.
>   That woman does look like me.

>   GARRETT
>   I'd say.

>   CORI
>   That's not me.

INT. GARRETT'S PANEL TRUCK, DIRT ROAD - DAY

Within a chilly silence, Garrett drives and Cori
stares ahead.

>   GARRETT
>   I'm an honest man. And a pacifist.
>   Assuming there is such a thing.

>   CORI
>   There isn't.

>   GARRETT
>   Not that I used to be. Even smart
>   people, Cori, can do stupid things.

He parks by the house, starts to exit. She grabs
his arm.

>   CORI
>   I swear, that wasn't me.

Garrett shakes off her grip.

>   GARRETT
>   One hundred percent trust is what I
>   give a person - until they lie to me.

He exits the truck, stops, returns to the window.

>   GARRETT
>   I don't know what you're up to. I
>   don't really care. And I sure as hell
>   don't want any part of it. You can
>   stay the night. But I want you out of
>   here in the morning.

INT. BEDROOM, GARRETT'S HOUSE - NIGHT

In the hills a coyote is HOWLING as Cori CRIES
into a pillow.

Alerted suddenly, she looks up. Professor Naught
is standing at the foot of her bed. She SCREAMS.
He places a finger to his lips, blows a kiss,
then vanishes.

There's a quiet KNOCKING. Her door opens.

>   GARRETT
>   Are you all right?

>   CORI
>   Not exactly.

>   GARRETT
>   May I come in?

He flicks on the light, looks around. He notices
her tears.

>   CORI
>   I thought I saw ... I was wrong.

>   GARRETT
>   Try trusting me. What is it?

>   CORI
>   I realized, I have nowhere else to
>   go. It's pathetic, really.

He walks into the bathroom, returns with a box
of tissues.

GARRETT
It's okay to cry, you know.

CORI
I did nothing wrong.

GARRETT
Be honest with me, Cori, or I'm not
about to help you.

CORI
Why would you want to?

He rubs his beard, sits down on the edge of the bed.

GARRETT
Because, you see, I've no place else
to go either.
          (slight smile)
You walked away from a jackpot. I'd
call that unusual. You never talked
to the police, did you? Tell me
what's going on.

She blows her nose.

CORI
You tell me.

GARRETT
Tell you what?

CORI
About you and Robert. You said he
talked to you. You should know.

GARRETT
Know what?

CORI
That I'm innocent. An art student.

> GARRETT

Right. And he was a pool hustler.
Hustling woman, like you, into bed.

> CORI

You're wrong. It was love. We were
going to get married. He said -

She freezes.

> CORI

Oh, shit. My sketchpad. With notes. I
dropped it when he was knifed.

> GARRETT

These men saw you?

> CORI

No, I mean - it was dark. Maybe.

Garrett strokes his beard, stands. She ventures
a hopeful smile when he returns after pacing to
sit back on the bed.

> GARRETT

Why go to a casino? Explain that.

> CORI

I can't. I was scared and confused. I
didn't know where to go. I wasn't
trying to win a jackpot! I panicked.

> GARRETT

That article said the police are
searching for you. Maybe they just
want to know if you're okay.

> CORI

That must be it.

She looks back with sad eyes, then gives a
playful smile.

> CORI
> Does this mean I can stay? I swear,
> I've been house trained.

Garrett's smile betrays him. His gruff exterior crumbles, replaced by a 'what-the-hell' prickly sarcasm.

> GARRETT
> You're quite a catch. Stay if you
> want. You'll be safe here.

> CORI
> What about those cowboys?

> GARRETT
> As far as they know, you're still my
> sister. Good night.

EXT. PORTICO, GARRETT'S HOUSE - LATE AT NIGHT

Cori holds her purse. She sneaks out the front door. She gets into her stolen car. The engine won't start.

> CORI
> Shit-shit-shit.

She goes to the panel truck, looking for keys. She notices a flickering light, like a signal, coming from the junkyard.

EXT. JUNKYARD, GARRETT'S PROPERTY - SAME

Cori investigates, creeping into the maze of demolished vehicles. She reaches a motor home where she saw the flickering light.

> CORI
> This is crazy. What am I doing?

She freezes.

CUT TO: GHOSTS OF BODIES INSIDE THE MANGLED CARS.

INT. MOTOR-HOME, GARRETT'S PROPERTY - SAME

Dover and Briggs observe Cori through their
night goggles.

> BRIGGS
> She's going to blow our cover.

> DOVER
> I had to distract her.

> BRIGGS
> What's she seeing? This is weird.
> I think she's completely lost it.

> DOVER
> (evasive)
> She's... enigmatic. High strung.

> BRIGGS
> Or strung-out.

> DOVER
> Do it. Hit the alarm.

EXT. JUNKYARD, GARRETT'S PROPERTY - SAME

The recorded GROWL of a bear startles Cori into
motion. She bangs her knee on a car bumper as
she scurries away.

EXT. PORTICO, GARRETT'S PROPERTY - SAME

Cori limps to the front door carrying her purse.

INT. GARRETT'S STUDIO - NEXT DAY, NOON

Cori enters with a slight limp and a sunny
smile. Garrett keeps working on Daphne, glancing
at her once or twice.

                    CORI
I thought I'd watch, maybe draw.

                    GARRETT
Pull a muscle getting out of bed?

                    CORI
I guess. Stupid me.

                    GARRETT
I don't charge admission. There's
sketch pads in that cabinet. Pens and
charcoal. Help yourself.

Cori looks at the figurine shrouded in a torrent
of motion.

                    GARRETT
Lost wax technique. Have you arrived
at a name for her yet?

                    CORI
No. But she intrigues me.

Garrett ignites the welding torch.

                    GARRETT
She's meant to. Remember not to stare
into the arc.

INT. GARRETT'S STUDIO - LATER

Cori sketches Garrett as he works on Daphne.

He resembles a warrior in battle as sparks fly,
popping and crackling. He removes his helmet.

                    CORI
She's beautiful, your Daphne.

                    GARRETT
Thank you.

                    CORI
          But a sad beauty.

                    GARRETT
          That too. Can I get you to model?

Cori stiffens.

                    GARRETT
          With your clothes on. To check on
          Daphne's proportions.

                    CORI
          What would I have to do?

                    GARRETT
          Hold those branches. So I can imagine
          you more easily as a tree. I promise,
          it won't hurt.

                    CORI
          Only my pride.

                    GARRETT
          Be proud. Daphne was.

She grabs the branches, twists her smile, then
her torso.

                    GARRETT
          Bend your neck. A bit more. Perfect.

                    CORI
          Do I resemble a tree?

                    GARRETT
          The most beautiful in the forest.

INT. GARRETT'S STUDIO - LATER

Cori, reseated, idly taps her pencil upon the
sketch pad.

                        CORI
When you're finished, do you plan to
put her in the garden to rust?

                        GARRETT
Occasionally I have a buyer.
Reluctantly I bid them farewell.

                        CORI
I heard a bear last night. I guess
they come around here.

                        GARRETT
Not usually.

                        CORI
Have you ever caught anyone living
out there in your junkyard?

                        GARRETT
Not yet. Why?

                        CORI
No reason.

Garrett lowers the shield over his face, then
raises it.

                        GARRETT
I thought we'd go to Virginia City.

                        CORI
Why? What's there?

                        GARRETT
History.

INT. MOTEL, NEVADA TOWN - MORNING

Pickard SCREAMS and wakes. Twisted up in the bed
sheets, his forehead is glistening with sweat.

EXT. SIDEWALK, NEVADA TOWN - MORNING

Pickard, in a silk suit, assesses this nothing
of a town.

INT. CAFE, NEVADA TOWN - SAME

Pickard grabs a few toothpicks at the counter
and puts them in his pocket. He takes a window
seat and opens a menu.

> ERIN
> Morning, handsome. Care for a cup?

> PICKARD
> That would be lovely, like you.

> ERIN
> Have you decided what you want?

He holds up a photo and looks at her name tag.

> PICKARD
> Have you seen this woman, Erin?

> ERIN
> What's she to you?

> PICKARD
> Wrong answer. Take a closer look.

> ERIN
> Are you a cop?

> PICKARD
> I'm a special investigator.

> ERIN
> I see lots of people come through.
> I'll give it some thought.

> PICKARD
> You do that, Erin. Careful thought.

Martino walks behind her and sits across from
Pickard.

                    MARTINO
        Miss, I'll take some of that.

Erin nervously overpours his coffee.

                    ERIN
        Sorry. I'll get you a new cup.

                    MARTINO
        Don't sweat it.

                    PICKARD
        We were discussing Corina.

                    MARTINO
        You know her?

                    ERIN
        No. Maybe. I -

                    PICKARD
        You can begin by telling us when you
        might have seen her. Today?

                    ERIN
        No.

                    PICKARD
        Yesterday?

                    ERIN
        The day before. I'm not sure.

                    PICKARD
        I'd appreciate any details upon your
        return. You deserve a tip.

He hands her fifty dollars. He then turns to
Martino.

                    PICKARD
          I'm ravenous. You?

                    MARTINO
          I'm always hungry.

Pickard touches and pats the bulge in his coat
pocket and grins.

                    PICKARD
          What a glorious day. I should shoot
          someone and make it perfect.

                    MARTINO
          Jeez, back off. I just want to eat.
          You, uh, sleep okay last night?

                    PICKARD
          Never better.

INT. GARRETT'S PANEL TRUCK, NEVADA - AFTERNOON

Garrett points to an abandoned mine on a barren
mountain as the road steepens, narrowing, rising
through a gorge.

                    CORI
          Robert told me you were a miner.

                    GARRETT
          Once upon a summer's dream.

                    CORI
          Did you find that precious stuff?

Garrett digs into his pants pocket and hands her
a gold nugget.

                    GARRETT
          Take a look.

                    CORI
          You dug this up?

                    GARRETT
It was given to me.

                    CORI
Given? What's it worth?

                    GARRETT
A hundred dollars. Maybe. Have it.

                    CORI
What's the catch?

                    GARRETT
It's meant to be given away. That's
what I was told, when given to me.

                    CORI
That must mean you have plenty more.

                    GARRETT
Gold is really not that precious.
Feel free to part with it anytime.

                    CORI
Don't count on it.

EXT. OVERVIEW OF VIRGINIA CITY - AFTERNOON

Old buildings, clustered like metamorphic rock
formations on a hill. Garrett's truck is seen
moving down its center.

INT. GARRETT'S PANEL TRUCK - SAME

Cori flips the nugget in her hand as she looks at -

Storefronts: Wild Bunch Souvenirs, Gold Rush
Jewelry, Mark Twain Ice Cream, Ponderosa Mine
Tours. The commercialization is pandemic.

EXT. SIDEWALK, VIRGINIA CITY - DUSK

Cori and Garrett sit on a bench eating ice cream cones.

                    CORI
        Why did we come so late?

                    GARRETT
        Shops will be closing soon, except
        for the bars. It'll be easier to
        imagine how this place used to be.

                    CORI
        What's the big attraction?

                    GARRETT
        A place to go, is all.

She smiles, forms a gun with her hand and aims
it at him.

                    CORI
        You and all the outlaws.

He snatches her fingers and tenderly gives them
a fleeting kiss.

                    GARRETT
        I prefer peace, not warfare. But
        nature was generally viewed back then
        as wild and up-for-grabs, to be raped
        and tamed, not adored.

                    CORI
        Like a woman.

He shrugs, ambivalent. He swallows the last of
his cone.

                    GARRETT
        Gunfights were surprisingly rare
        considering the influx of people and
        all that sought after metal pulled
        from the ground. Troublemakers got
        lynched from headframes inside the
        mines by a committee called the 601.

                    CORI
The town's welcome wagon?

                    GARRETT
          (off her dry humor)
          Are you ready for a cocktail at the
          Bucket of Blood saloon?

                    CORI
How romantic.

They stand. She fires her two-fingered gun at him.

                    GARRETT
          (takes it with a smile)
          It's strange how these outcasts have
          come to be viewed. As if mythical.

He points to a Wanted Poster of Billy the Kid, a
souvenir displayed in a storefront window. It's
the same face of the menacing GHOST now blocking
Cori's path on the sidewalk.

                    GARRETT
          A pathetic creep. His victims were
          mostly unarmed or shot from ambush.
          Psychopaths, most of these outlaws.
          Not the likes of anyone I'd ever come
          to admire, I can assure you.

The GHOST disperses. Cori, disconcerted, walks on.

INT. CABIN IN WOODS, NEVADA - AFTERNOON

Pickard is in a chair. Erin McBride opens the
door, flips on a light switch, and is grabbed
from behind. Her SCREAM is muffled by a hand.

                    PICKARD
          Same dance I saw on Wild Kingdom.

                    MARTINO
Fuck off.

>   PICKARD
> Erin, you need to be quiet. Can I
> trust you to behave?

She nods nervously. Martino takes his hand off
her mouth.

Pickard places a toothpick between his teeth.

>   PICKARD
> That's my girl.

>   ERIN
> Are you here to rob me?

>   PICKARD
> No. Not to rob you.

>   ERIN
> I don't have much. I mean, you can
> see I'm a - a photographer.

On the walls are photos of trees buried in fog,
a torrent of water circling rocks, a lone spider
in its web.

>   PICKARD
> You left without informing me. That
> was very naughty of you, Erin.

>   ERIN
> He has no phone, or address. I need
> to sit down.

>   PICKARD
> Do I make you nervous?

>   ERIN
> He lives up in the hills. And it's —
> it's difficult to find.

>   PICKARD
> Then you shall be our guide.

                    ERIN
                 (alarmed)
        No. I can draw you a map.

                   PICKARD
        I'd rather you show me.

                    ERIN
        I have a date tonight.

                   PICKARD
        You'll be forgiven.

Pickard SPRINGS forward to stand. He holds out
his hand and pulls Erin to her feet. Martino has
the door held open.

                    ERIN
        I need to use the bathroom.

                   PICKARD
        You'll have to wait.

                    ERIN
        I don't think I can.

                   PICKARD
        It's a new Mercedes. You'd better.

INT. BLACK MERCEDES, CABIN IN WOODS - SAME

Pickard drives. Erin is beside him. Martino is
seated in the back. A car with police lights and
a door insignia emerges from the trees. The
driver waves and then begins to follow.

INT. BUCKET OF BLOOD SALOON - DUSK

Garrett and Cori sit at the bar. The bartender,
ALEX, 30, has a long mustache. He tips his hat,
surprised to see Cori.

> ALEX
> Kyle, you son of a dog. Don't tell me
> she's with you. Are you?

> CORI
> I'm afraid so.

They all LAUGH. Alex extends a hand to be shaken
by Cori.

> GARRETT
> Alex, meet Cori. Two Margaritas,
> virgin. Here. I've been meaning to
> mail this to you.

He detaches a key from a ring of others, tosses
it to Alex.

> ALEX
> You still ski?

> GARRETT
> I gave it up. No interest. You're
> welcome to whatever's inside.

> ALEX
> I'll have a look. Thanks.

Alex omits the Tequila and switches on a blender.

> ALEX
> We used to burn up the slopes.

Cori is believing none of this.

> GARRETT
> I need to use the head.

Garrett excuses himself. He leaves his keys on
the bar. A customer calls Alex away. Cori hears
a VOICE -

>   MALE (O.C.)
> Make your break. Now. Move!

Cori picks up Garrett's keys, exits through a back door.

INT. GARRETT'S TRUCK, VIRGINIA CITY - NIGHT

Cori starts to drive away. Through the wind-shield she sees an ANGEL standing in the center of a dark deserted street.

Cori brakes. The transparent ANGEL is glowing. It's the same woman she saw in the cafe parking lot and inside the casino.

>   GHOST (V.O.)
>   Stay.

>   CORI
> You left me, Mother!

The ANGEL dissolves. Cori sits dazed. She exits the truck - realizing the truck is still parked where it was.

>   CORI
> What the hell just happened?

INT. BUCKET OF BLOOD SALOON - SAME

Cori reseats herself, looking distraught and defensive. She DROPS Garrett's keys on the bar countertop.

>   CORI
> You shouldn't leave your keys lying
> around on the bar.

>   GARRETT
> Thanks for watching them for me.

                    CORI
         No problem.

Alex slides her a Margarita. Her hand trembles
as she lifts her drink.

                    ALEX
         Are you okay?

                    CORI
         Why wouldn't I be?

                    GARRETT
              (at Alex)
         I told you. Feisty.

                    CORI
         I went for a walk. I got cold.

                    ALEX
         Okay.

                    CORI
         You look familiar.

                    ALEX
         It's probably the mustache.

She studies their smiles with suspicion.

                    CORI
         Is this a prank?

                    ALEX
         Who knows. The world is constantly
         messing with my mind.

Alex's eyes linger on her. He leaves to serve
customers.

                    CORI
         What's up with him?

GARRETT
He said you remind him of someone.

CORI
I get that line a lot. You've known
him, what, a long time?

GARRETT
Long enough. He's a good man.
Considering I knocked out his teeth -
and that we're still friends.

CORI
What provoked you to do that?

GARRETT
I was drunk. It doesn't take much
reason, more the lack of it.

CORI
So you were an outlaw.

GARRETT
Reckless is all. I was a bartender.
Worked here. Sorta like hiring a
pyromaniac to work the fire hoses.

CORI
You were that good.

GARRETT
A natural. Half the saloon burned
down. That was in 1875. Wasn't my
fault. A cow kicked over a lantern.
Not all you see here is authentic.

Cori twists her mouth and surveys the rows of
slot machines.

CORI
The one-armed bandits gave it away.

                    GARRETT
That rush for gold has never left.

                    ALEX
          (overhears)
The perils from mining are legion.
Like the Grosh brothers, who never
lived to profit from the bonanza of
silver they unearthed here. One of
them puts a pick through his foot and
dies from blood-poisoning. The other
one, he dies from frostbite.

                    GARRETT
Even Henry Comstock, for whom this
lode was named. After bragging about
selling his claim for thousands, he
realizes later it was worth millions.
He shot himself in the head.

Alex twirls his hat theatrically and gives her a
rueful smile.

                    ALEX
Greed can mess with your head.

                    GARRETT
And summon the demons too.

Unnerved by their talk, Cori tries to appear unfazed.

                    CORI
What about ghosts?

                    ALEX
Oh, sure. Ask KG. Ghosts are all
around us. But mostly in the mind.
Apparitions are funny that way.

INT. PICKARD'S MERCEDES, DIRT ROAD - DUSK

Pickard is driving. He bites and wiggles his
toothpick.

CUT TO: THE METAL SNAKE COMING INTO VIEW OVER
THE ROAD.

                    PICKARD
          Now that is fucking bizarre.

They pass the HUNK OF JUNK sign and more sculptures.

                    PICKARD
          Erin, do you believe in luck? I do.
          But I prefer to manufacture mine.

The road curves. The view changes to fields of
rusted cars.

                    PICKARD
          I believe we've reached the end of
          the earth. Place looks like hell.

Erin stares, equating her situation as just that
- HELL.

                    PICKARD
          I'd be dead, if I had failed to
          control recent events. And this would
          not be happening. In other words,
          this is your bad luck.

Martino GRUNTS a half laugh.

                    PICKARD
          It's the reason I stay connected.
          I know a variety of people and they
          respect me. They know they'll be
          rewarded. I can be very generous.

He points with his toothpick at the junkyard of cars.

                    PICKARD
          Darwin was a genius. Do you realize
          only the successful have littered the
          world with its bones. The failures,
          they haven't left us shit.

Garrett's house and art studio come into view.

Pickard drives off the dirt road and parks to be
hidden behind a cluster of tall bushes.

> PICKARD
> Regarding luck, Erin. One of my
> people, he gets imprisoned with this
> kid from the ghetto. A gang-banger
> who mentions his sister. She works on
> the other side. Not dead. A fucking
> Fed. Whose division is weapons and
> narcotics. My department. If you
> hadn't guessed, I'm not a cop.

> MARTINO
> No shit.

> PICKARD
> So, anyway, I investigate. You see,
> with my paid informants, the data
> trails, and strokes of good fortune -
> I stay alive.

> ERIN
> That's his studio. He's an artist.

He strokes her bare thigh and she shudders.

> PICKARD
> I want to believe you're telling me
> the truth, Erin.

> ERIN
> I am.

> PICKARD
> Choose a door.

INT. RANGE ROVER, VIRGINIA CITY - NIGHT

Dover is typing on a laptop computer as Briggs
watches the street.

                    BRIGGS
He didn't take the bait. Pickard's
probably left the country.

                    DOVER
He's here. Somewhere close.

                    BRIGGS
Slipperier than an eel. Pure slime.

Dover is focussed on the computer. Briggs is fuming.

                    BRIGGS
We just sit as he assaults women? I
think he knew we were watching him.

                    DOVER
He likes to taunt.
          (at Briggs)
No, I did not enjoy the exhibition.

Briggs reacts as if he can read her thoughts.

                    BRIGGS
I never said you did.

                    DOVER
You didn't have to.

                    BRIGGS
We should have killed him then and
there while we had the chance.

                    DOVER
It's not that simple. Don't forget,
he travels with an entourage.

                    BRIGGS
So do we.

                    DOVER
We need to know what he's planning
and stop it from happening.

                    DOVER (cont'd)
                  (into his phone)
         Ramos, what's the status?

INT. RAMOS' VEHICLE, GARRETT'S PROPERTY - SAME

A phone is held to Ramos' head - also a gun.

                      RAMOS
         Nothing to report, Chief.

INT. RANGE ROVER, VIRGINIA CITY - SAME

Dover rubs his eyes.

                      DOVER
         He's here, I can feel him.

                      BRIGGS
         He'd be a fool to stay.

                      DOVER
         He doesn't think like we do. He
         thinks he can outsmart us all.

Dover reacts to something on his computer.

                      DOVER
         The police found Naught. They sent a
         video. It's downloading.

INT. FLUORESCENT-LIT ROOM, VIDEO

CLOSE ON Naught's face, then pulling back to
reveal he is bound to a chair with duct tape.

                      NAUGHT
         Bravo. You escaped the trap. For the
         record, my intent was never to harm,
         only to enlighten the world. And for
         that, as thanks, I am to be cremated.
         But first, burn this into memory, you
         who are but a little boy lost.

Naught is doused with gasoline. The ASSASSIN's
hand lights a match - igniting Naught whose
stoic last words are -

          NAUGHT
     'Do what you will, this life is a
     fiction, made up of contradiction.'
     William Blake, my dear boy.

INT. BUCKET OF BLOOD SALOON - SAME

          CORI
     What did Alex mean by that?

          GARRETT
     An encounter I had. I saw a ghost.
     Alex believes it was a delusion.

          CORI
     You were drunk.

          GARRETT
     You catch on fast. I got thrown in
     jail. My cell mates blindsided me
     with punches. They kicked me hard in
     the groin, my ribs, head and face. It
     was a miracle I lived.

          CORI
     Is that how you got those scars?

He winces, looks away into the darkness outside.

          GARRETT
     It's their laughter I can't forget.
     Pat Garrett was the sheriff who
     killed Billy the Kid. He was quoted
     as saying this about that - Kid. How
     he ate and laughed, drank and
     laughed, rode and laughed, talked and
     laughed, fought and laughed, killed
     and laughed.

CLOSE ON his pained expression, his facial scars.

                  GARRETT
      Laughter arises from having fun.
      While these men were beating me to
      death, I kept thinking about Billy
      the Kid. His constant laughing. Had
      to have been the same kind I heard.

His anguish is deep. Cori touches his wrist. He
returns a smile.

                  GARRETT
      Thanks. When did you first realize
      there was a God, Cori?

Cori reacts with suspicion, surprised by the question.

                  CORI
      Never. Unlucky, I guess, to have
      missed being kicked in the head.

                  GARRETT
         (humored)
      It's what you feel in your heart.

                  CORI
      I don't know what you mean.

                  GARRETT
      Sure you do.

                  CORI
         (annoyed)
      Honest. I don't.

                  GARRETT
      Recall a time when you weren't aware
      of that beautiful face, or people
      telling you who you should be, maybe
      the first time you realized you were
      alive, staring at the sky, saying to
      yourself — this is who I am. Try.

She returns his stare and narrows her eyes.

>   CORI
> You have this bad habit, remember?

As he grins and looks away, Cori's eyes wander overhead to gaze into the glow of a red chandelier.

>   CORI
> Euphoria. That's the name my father
> wanted to give me. I was told this by
> my mother. She fought him and they
> compromised on Corina. I was seven
> when she died. Mysteriously. I wanted
> to die too. I blamed my father. I
> kept trying to leave.

>   GARRETT
> You ran away?

>   CORI
> It didn't help. He always found me.
> I accused him of killing her.
>   (tears form)
> He slapped me. Told me I was smart,
> like her. And hard to love. Right
> about then I knew there was no God.

>   GARRETT
> You're wrong, Cori. When you feel
> that kind of hurt, you're feeling God
> too. Otherwise, you'd have felt
> nothing. Maybe laughed instead.

Cori stares at Garrett. He gives a warm smile.

>   GARRETT
> I'm sorry. Care to dance?

>   CORI
> There's no music.

                    GARRETT
        At the Silver Queen. They have a band
        starting about now. Hungry?

EXT. ART STUDIO, GARRETT'S PROPERTY - DUSK

Martino slides open the door as Pickard aims a
semiautomatic.

                    ERIN
        He's not here.

                    PICKARD
        Erin, do I look blind?

EXT. PORTICO, GARRETT'S PROPERTY - SAME

Pickard regards the metal sculpture of a large
sleeping woman.

                    PICKARD
        She'd be one hell of a fuck.

INT. LIVING ROOM, GARRETT'S HOME - SAME

Pickard eyes the wall paintings of gods looking
down at them.

                    MARTINO
        I'll check upstairs.

                    PICKARD
        Remain an asset, Erin. Where is he?

                    ERIN
        Is this about Cori, his sister?

Pickard aims his gun from the gods to her forehead.

                    PICKARD
        Sister? You said you knew nothing.

                    ERIN
I met her, only briefly, I swear!

                    PICKARD
I know a lot about you, Erin. You're
a whore. That's a fact.

                    ERIN
          (startled)
No. I'm not. Anymore.

                    PICKARD
Maybe I fucked you at Mustang Ranch.
Did they put you out to pasture?

                    ERIN
I'm a photographer.

                    PICKARD
And a waitress. Let me give you a
tip. People don't change that much.
You're still servicing customers.

                    ERIN
          (backs away)
KG, I mean Kyle, he got me to quit.

                    PICKARD
Did he.

                    ERIN
He's a good man.

He knocks over a lamp to the floor - EXPLODING
its globe.

                    ERIN
He could be outside. He built a
garden. And — and there's a pond.

                    MARTINO
Upstairs is empty!

                    PICKARD
          Erin and I are going outside.

EXT. PORTICO, GARRETT'S PROPERTY - SAME

Erin BUMPS backwards into the metal sculpture as
Pickard RIPS the shoulder strap on her dress.

                    ERIN
          What are you doing?

                    PICKARD
          Having fun. You were once a beauty
          queen too. A pageant finalist.

                    ERIN
          How - how did you know that?

                    PICKARD
          And a cheerleader. Kicking up those
          long legs. Showing off your panties.

                    ERIN
          Don't, please.

                    PICKARD
          Show me.

                    ERIN
          What?

                    PICKARD
          That garden. I want to see it.

EXT. MAIN STREET, VIRGINIA CITY - NIGHT

Garrett stops to stare at the sky full of stars.

Cori is alarmed, entranced by GHOSTS animating
the town.

                    CORI
          This is unbelievable.

                    GARRETT
          It can be beautiful, this world. The
          Silver Queen's this way.

INT. SILVER QUEEN SALOON - LATER

Garrett and Cori sit at a table with food and
sodas. A band is playing country blues MUSIC.
She appears distracted.

                    GARRETT
          Are you enjoying yourself?

                    CORI
          You're the mind reader.

                    GARRETT
          It's more fun with a date. I mean,
          having a woman to dance with.

                    CORI
          Is that what I am?

                    GARRETT
          You're not a woman?

Cori ignores his quip and toothpicks a mini hot
dog appetizer.

Garrett is puzzled by her frozen stare at the
appetizer.

CUT TO: CORI HIDING THE CYLINDRICAL DEVICE IN
THE WOODS.

                    GARRETT
          Care for a spin on the dance floor?

                    CORI
          I have a confession to make.

                    GARRETT
          Don't tell me you're not a woman.

                    CORI
Something's wrong with me.

                    GARRETT
Could you be more specific?

                    CORI
I'm hearing voices. Seeing things.

                    GARRETT
What sort of things?

                    CORI
Ghosts.

INT. SILVER QUEEN SALOON - SAME

Dover is seated at a corner table with Briggs.
Feeling sick and exhausted, he shuts his eyes.
He MUTTERS incoherent words. She nudges him.

                    BRIGGS
You're talking out loud.

                    DOVER
I must've caught a bug. I feel awful.
How are you doing?

                    BRIGGS
Better than you.
       (direct look)
Is this about us?

                    DOVER
Nadine, why not give it a try.

                    BRIGGS
It would never work.

                    DOVER
       (self-deprecating)
I'll try to perform better in bed.

             BRIGGS
You were wonderful. I wasn't.

             DOVER
Why did you cry?

INT. SILVER QUEEN SALOON - SAME

Seated at their table, Cori listens intently to
Garrett.

             GARRETT
Did you know jellyfish, invisible in
the ocean, can flare up and glow -
suddenly become visible?

             CORI
Meaning?

             GARRETT
They have bioluminescence. They use
it to scare predators and seek help.

             CORI
Like these ghosts? How do you mean?

             GARRETT
You're seeing into another realm.
    (smiles, nods)
I'd pick you, if I was a ghost.

             CORI
Are you saying I'm possessed?

             GARRETT
No. But able to register them. And
they know it. It's as if you've
become like, some kind of magnet.

             CORI
Gee, that's reassuring.

A dark winged humanlike entity stands over Dover.

Cori is more curious than alarmed, observing
this ghost.

                    GARRETT
          Earth to Cori. You still with me?

She blinks, realizes the question.

                    CORI
          I hid something on your property the
          day I came here. A cylinder about the
          size of these hot dogs.
               (she studies him)
          You knew about this, didn't you?

                    GARRETT
          Not really.

                    CORI
          Bad answer.

Cori pushes away. Garrett takes hold of her arm.

                    GARRETT
          FYI - we're being watched.

Cori glances at Dover and Briggs who avert their eyes.

                    GARRETT
          My turn to confess.

                    CORI
          Who are they?

                    GARRETT
          CIA.

                    CORI
          And you?

                    GARRETT
          I'm not. Anymore. I got involved the
          same time you did.

                    CORI
What are you talking about? Are you
saying we knew each other. Wait.
          (studies him)
Did you know I'd show up here?

                    GARRETT
I wasn't totally surprised.

                    CORI
Those cowboys. CIA?

                    GARRETT
It's not like you trusted me either.

                    CORI
What else have I missed?

                    GARRETT
You honestly don't know?

                    CORI
Know what?

                    GARRETT
          (realizing)
My God, you don't know. Do you? You
were involved in a sting operation to
entrap Pickard.

                    CORI
Who?

                    GARRETT
International terrorist.

                    CORI
My mind isn't right. A car hit me.
And my head struck the pavement.

                    GARRETT
They claim you double-crossed Robert
and stole classified data.

                    CORI
No.

                    GARRETT
Except I don't buy it either.

                    CORI
The CIA think I'm involved?

                    GARRETT
You are involved.

                    CORI
I'm not. I - I tried to stop him,
I think. I found this device in my
purse. I buried it in the woods.

                    GARRETT
What else do you remember?

                    CORI
Blood pouring over my hands. I saw
his face in the bathroom mirror. As a
ghost. As if he was already dead.

                    GARRETT
Robert?

                    CORI
I would have never betrayed him.

He studies her with an intense stare.

                    GARRETT
I thought you were dead.

                    CORI
What do you mean?

                    GARRETT
As in deceased. Why don't we talk
about this on the dance floor.

                    CORI
      No.

He cocks his head at the CIA agents.

                    CORI
      Okay. Sure.

INT. SILVER QUEEN SALOON - LATER

Cori and Garrett dance to slow MUSIC. In the
background Dover and Briggs observe them from a
corner table.

                    CORI
      I was in a coma. From a car crash.
      That's what I was told. Most of my
      memories, they're vague. Or gone.

                    GARRETT
      You have an impressive IQ.

                    CORI
      How would you know that?

                    GARRETT
      You were tested.

                    CORI
      When?

                    GARRETT
      Nine years ago. A research project on
      the paranormal. You were there. Along
      with Robert. Him, Dover. Also Alex.
      And Pickard, with a different name.

Cori stops moving.

                    GARRETT
      You remember none of this? The
      biofeedback. Psychic regressions.
      Or the chemicals we all took?

                    CORI
          I don't take drugs or chemicals.

                    GARRETT
          You did. We all did.

                    CORI
          Tell me.

                    GARRETT
          The lab rats, meaning us, started
          experiencing bad reactions.

                    CORI
          How bad?

                    GARRETT
          Someone died.

                    CORI
          I'd say that's bad.

                    GARRETT
          When Rob told me you were alive,
          I didn't believe him at first. It
          didn't seem possible. Then -

                    CORI
          Wait. What, I died?

The MUSIC stops. Garrett and Cori are left standing.

                    GARRETT
          Apparently not. You went into a coma.
          Then your heart stopped. Cardiac
          arrest. I attended your funeral.

Livelier MUSIC begins but they continue dancing
slowly.

                    CORI
          Robert was killed right after I saw
          his face, as a ghost, in the mirror.

                    GARRETT
It's a time delay. We all have it.

                    CORI
We all have what?

                    GARRETT
A slight edge over time.

                    CORI
That night you heard me scream, I saw
my father again, as a ghost.

                    GARRETT
You're sure it wasn't a dream?

                    CORI
I was awake. He stood at the foot of
the bed. Then he slowly faded.

                    GARRETT
Was there any sort of communication?

                    CORI
He blew me kiss.

They continue dancing. Cori begins to cry.

                    GARRETT
We'll figure this out together.

                    CORI
You don't understand. Robert, he -

                    GARRETT
You were in love.

                    CORI
It doesn't matter now.

                    GARRETT
It matters.

INT. GARRETT'S PANEL TRUCK, CARSON CITY - LATER

Garrett is driving as Cori stares out the side window.

                    CORI
          It feels strange to be dead.

                    GARRETT
          You're not. You're alive.

                    CORI
          Are any of my memories even real?

                    GARRETT
          Your mind's been tampered with.

                    CORI
          My whole life feels fake.

                    GARRETT
          The research was government funded.

                    CORI
          Why did we do it? It's stupid.

                    GARRETT
          Your father was offering us the full
          powers of our minds.

                    CORI
          And we bought that crap?

                    GARRETT
          He was very convincing.

INT. GARRETT'S PANEL TRUCK, PAST CARSON CITY - SAME

Garrett continues to drive. Cori rolls the gold nugget in her palm.

                    CORI
          How can my memories not be true?

                    GARRETT
I don't know. Why do we exist?

                    CORI
You're a big help.

                    GARRETT
Your mind impressed me. All of us.
Only you were able to solve these
incredibly complex equations.

                    CORI
I don't remember any of that.

                    GARRETT
We were conducting an out-of-body
experiment when, you know.

                    CORI
I died?

                    GARRETT
Your beauty. That impressed me too.

                    CORI
          (dawns on her)
Wait. Were you in love with me?

                    GARRETT
Along with everyone else.

                    CORI
What made you volunteer?

                    GARRETT
Same reason a moth seeks the flame.

                    CORI
To get burned?

                    GARRETT
For the illumination.

EXT. GARRETT'S TRUCK, NEVADA MOUNTAINS - LATER

An aerial view of the truck moving uphill under a full moon.

                    GARRETT (V.O.)
          I was also drawn by greed.

                    CORI (V.O.)
          Greed for what?

                    GARRETT
          Power. To impress others. You.
                    (glances at her)
          It's amazing what a woman can do to
          the dynamics of a group of men. That
          was part of Naught's plan, I think.

INT. GARRETT'S TRUCK, NEVADA MOUNTAIN - SAME

Garrett SHIFTS into a higher gear.

                    GARRETT
          He gave us new lives then scattered
          us like seeds in the wind. As if to
          see who took root. Did good or bad.

                    CORI
          You lost me.

                    GARRETT
          I did.
                    (downshifts)
          I can't fathom why Pickard turned
          into this bad seed. And, all of it.

                    CORI
          What?

                    GARRETT
          Became so wicked. Whatever this thing
          is we have, it gives us an advantage.
          Yet, it's affected us differently.

Garrett slows the truck, pulls off to the side of the road.

He exits, Cori gets out too. They stare at the empty road.

                    GARRETT
          A silver sedan. Toyota. Brand new.

Cori frowns then sees the car appear and PASS them on the way uphill. Garrett shrugs before returning to the truck.

INT. SEQUENCE OF CASINOS AND BARS - (FLASHBACK)

Garrett, Robert and Alex are seen drinking and gambling at a blackjack table.

                    GARRETT (V.O.)
          I began drinking too much, shooting
          pool, gambling. I decided to profit
          from this gift we'd received.
                    (hard shift)
          I was mad. You were dead. Why not get
          rich as a consolation. The casinos
          didn't know how we were cheating
          them. But they knew.

INT. CASINO BACK ROOM - (FLASHBACK)

Garrett is threatened by men, STRUCK in the face.

                    CORI (V.O.)
          Like when I won that jackpot?

                    GARRETT (V.O.)
          You controlled the outcome.

INT. BARROOM, RENO - (FLASHBACK)

Garrett, Stikes and Alex are playing billiards when they start to argue then FIGHT.

                        GARRETT (V.O.)
          I drank myself into oblivion - I
          suppose in an attempt to kill off
          what I'd become. One night I got into
          an argument with Rob and Alex over
          you. We fought hard.

Garrett CRASHES through a storefront window onto
the sidewalk.

                        CORI (V.O.)
          Wait. You were fighting over me?

INT. BUCKET OF BLOOD SALOON - NIGHT

Alex is seated at a table talking with Osaki
when surprised by two men entering.

                        ALEX
          The door was locked. We're closed.

MAN #1 holds a gas can. MAN #2 holds a silencer.

                        ALEX
          Is this a joke?

                        MAN #2
          My boss wants you disappeared.

                        ALEX
          Hey, you have the wrong guy.

                        MAN #2
          Alex Thursten. That's you.

                        OSAKI
          If it's money you want -

Osaki is SHOT twice in the chest. Alex is then
SHOT in the head.

INT. GARRETT'S TRUCK, MOUNTAIN HIGHWAY - LATER

Garrett and Cori are engaged in a heated dispute.

          CORI
Wrong! Love makes you stupid.

          GARRETT
Love is like art. A necessity.

          CORI
Something you would know. Not me.

          GARRETT
Cori, there's more to lose when you
love someone.

          CORI
Don't tell me about loss. My mother
died from abuse. And my father loved
me short of raping me! All the while
telling me how special he'd make me.

Garrett slows, stops the truck off the highway.

          CORI
Don't stop on my account. I'm good.

          GARRETT
Cori, calm down. It'll be okay.

          CORI
Then you're a fool. Because I am
good. I'm very good — at lying.

          GARRETT
Like you've been lying all along.

          CORI
Fuck you!

She wildly slaps him, expecting him to hit back.
Instead, he's distracted by something outside.

                    GARRETT
Vandals damaged my road marker.

                    CORI
I see we're almost home. Will the CIA
be joining us for a nightcap?

                    GARRETT
I'll just drive and give you all the
space you need.

INT. TRUCK, DRIVEWAY GARRETT'S PROPERTY - SAME

Silence, then Garrett begins to exit. Cori grabs
his arm.

                    CORI
I'm sorry I hit you. Trusting people
doesn't come easy for me.

                    GARRETT
How's that lying business coming?

                    CORI
You've been nice to me. And I'm not -
I'm not used to nice.

                    GARRETT
God only knows what your father put
you through, Cori. I can't tell you
who you are or how to be. But you are
beautiful - on the inside too. Those
windows to your soul? I can see you.
You're a good person.

                    CORI
Were you really in love with me?

                    GARRETT
Unrequited. It doesn't matter.

                    CORI
It matters.

EXT. GARRETT'S STUDIO - SAME

Garret and Cori stop to look around at the trees
swaying and sculptures RATTLING in the WIND
under a full moon.

                    CORI
          I don't like being spied upon.

                    GARRETT
          They're here for our protection.

                    CORI
          I meant the ghosts.

                    GARRETT
          Maybe they're here to protect us too.

                    CORI
          Don't get your hopes up.

                    GARRETT
          You'll like my version of an Irish
          Cream. It will, however, require some
          trust on your part.

                    CORI
          I trust you. Somehow.

INT. RANGE ROVER, GARRETT'S PROPERTY - NIGHT

Briggs is driving. Dover is hunched over in the
passenger seat.

INT. MOTOR-HOME, GARRETT'S PROPERTY - SAME

Dover, feverish, drops onto a bed. Briggs locks
the door.

                    DOVER (V.O.)
          Rome fell this way. Barbarians at the
          gates. Glory gone. Sold cheap for a
          pile of scrap-metal dreams.

INSERT SERIES OF IMAGES - ANCIENT ROME, THE
FORUM, CAESAR STABBED BY SENATORS, BRIGGS SHOT
IN THE HEAD.

BACK TO SCENE

> DOVER
> Briggs!

She approaches with concern and puzzlement.

> DOVER
> I thought. Nothing. I'm okay.

> BRIGGS
> You need rest. I need some air.

EXT. MOTOR-HOME, JUNKYARD - SAME

Briggs holds night goggles. The sea of junk is
overwhelming. She KICKS a headlight which ROLLS
like a dislodged eyeball.

The strong wind streaks tears from her eyes.

> BRIGGS
> God, please, forgive me. I'll make
> things right. I will.

She hears a NOISE. The sound of Garrett's studio
door sliding open.

Magnified in the goggles, Cori exits the studio,
then enters the house. She returns holding a
towel and items bundled inside.

INT. MOTOR-HOME, GARRETT'S PROPERTY - SAME

Briggs enters and Dover LURCHES forward aiming
his gun.

> BRIGGS
> Hold your fire partner, it's me.

                    DOVER
                (falls back)
        Now I can die a happy man.

                    BRIGGS
        Videri carried something into the
        studio. I thought I'd investigate.

                    DOVER
        No word from Osaki? Anyone?

                    BRIGGS
        Negative.

                    DOVER
        Did you send the signal?

                    BRIGGS
        It's sent. Do you feel any better?

                    DOVER
        Like Alexander. I'm great.

                    BRIGGS
        Alexander?

                    DOVER
        He never lost a battle, except one.
        In Babylon. His body was attacked by
        a viral influenza. I'll probably die
        the same. From this damned flu bug.

                    BRIGGS
        Don't be morbid.

        They both react to a CLANGING outside.

                    BRIGGS
        The wind is blowing hard.

                    DOVER
        Be careful.

                    BRIGGS
        I'm a big girl. A warrior too.

Briggs looks out the windshield, then opens the
door. She's YANKED outside. Pickard comes inside
holding a silencer.

                    PICKARD
        Don't! Drop it!

Briggs is PUSHED inside by Martino. She avoids
Dover's eyes.

Toothpick in mouth, Pickard forces the gun into
Briggs' hand.

                    PICKARD
        You get to be his executioner.

                    DOVER
        Nadine, what the -

                    PICKARD
        We purchased her cheap.

                    BRIGGS
        They have my family!

Martino prods her. She adjusts the gun, gripping
it with her finger on the trigger.

                    DOVER
        I don't believe this.

                    PICKARD
        Your girl has been a big help.

                    DOVER
        Seven agents died for Christsake!

                    MARTINO
        Thirteen now, once we include you.

>   BRIGGS
>   No one was supposed to die! I'm
>   sorry. I do love you. I <u>do</u>.

She spins to shoot Pickard. He SHOOTS her.

Dover's POV: deja vu of Briggs SHOT in the head.

>   PICKARD
>   Submit to the fact, Dover, my genes
>   proved to be superior.

>   DOVER
>   You're a loser. You kill people.

He SHOOTS a bullet into Dover's upper thigh.

>   PICKARD
>   Often for pleasure. Has my angel been
>   good, or is she misbehaving?

>   DOVER
>   You think I'd tell you anything?

>   PICKARD
>   To save the family jewels, yes.

Dover dives for his gun. He's SHOT in the arm
and falls back.

>   DOVER
>   She has nothing you want. That device
>   is a fake. It's a decoy.

>   PICKARD
>   That's not what I wanted to hear.
>   You will now suffer for those lies.

Pickard SHOOTS Dover in each knee cap, then both
his elbows.

He removes the toothpick from his mouth.

> PICKARD
> You were never destined to be great.
> Only to die in this shithole. Me, I
> gave up being a lab rat nine fucking
> years ago.

Dover's POV: Pickard, as a giant, holding a tiny
wooden sword pinched between his thumb and index
finger and pointed at him.

> PICKARD
> Instead I decided to become a god.

INT. GARRETT'S STUDIO - LATER

The forge is heating. Cori touches the figurine
bound in an atmospheric swirl. Garrett hands her
a mug. She takes a sip.

> CORI
> Ummm, this is good. Very good.

> GARRETT
> Ambrosia. A gift from the gods.

She smiles, then looks back at the figurine.

> GARRETT
> Do you have a name for her yet?

> CORI
> I shouldn't, she's yours.

> GARRETT
> I value your thoughts.

> CORI
> Redemption. That's who she is.

> GARRETT
> I knew you'd be the one to figure it
> out. She's baffled me for weeks.

Cori sets down her mug, approaches him, puts her
arms around his neck and gives him a playful
kiss - but is unexpectedly drawn into a longer
one, then pushes away.

                    GARRETT
          What was that for?

                    CORI
          For valuing my thoughts. And for
          putting up with me.

Cori steps back to frame him within her fingers.

                    CORI
          Will you let me do something to you?

                    GARRETT
          Depends. Will it hurt?

                    CORI
          I'll try to be gentle. Wait here.

INT. GARRETT'S STUDIO - MINUTES LATER

Cori returns holding a towel. Wrapped within it
are scissors, razor, mirror, and shaving cream.
Garrett scratches his beard warily.

                    CORI
          A little makeover.

                    GARRETT
          I've become attached to this beard.

                    CORI
          It'll be fun. I promise.

                    GARRETT
          So long as you promise.

                    CORI
          Take a seat. You can trust me.

INT. GARRETT'S STUDIO - LATER

Cori snips away, cutting off clumps of beard.

                    GARRETT
          You've done this before?

                    CORI
          First time.

She makes an inept face. He laughs, shuts his eyes.

                    GARRETT
          I'm not amused.

She squirts and spreads shaving cream over the
closely-trimmed hairs. His bristles CRACKLE from
the razor as Cori shaves his skin smooth. Once
done, she rubs her finger across his upper lip
and leans in close with a kiss.

                    CORI
          Feel any different?

                    GARRETT
          You must have shaved too.

Cori covers his face with the towel and wipes
away the foam.

She admires his ruggedly handsome features.

                    GARRETT
          Is it safe to open my eyes?

Cori has placed a foam mustache across her upper
lip. He LAUGHS.

Garrett stops her hand from holding up a mirror
to his face.

                    GARRETT
          I'd rather see myself through you.

                    CORI
     I'm impressed with my work.

Her fingers touch the scar that extends from his
mouth to his jaw.

                  GARRETT
     An angry red line last time I saw it.

                    CORI
     Less angry, more gentle.

He stops her hand from touching the scar across
the bridge of his nose.

                    CORI
     You don't need to hide.

                  GARRETT
     Who said I was hiding?

                    CORI
     Now look who's lying?

Cori stands and unbuttons her jeans. She crosses
her arms and pulls her sweater over her head to
reveal a naked torso.

                    CORI
     You get to do something to me.
     Unless you'd like me to stop.

                  GARRETT
     God, no. Proceed. I approve.

Cori lowers her jeans, kicks them at him. She
toys with her panties before bringing them down.
She picks up the shaving cream and SQUIRTS him
with foam as he reaches for her.

                    CORI
     Who said you are allowed to touch?
     I want you to paint me.

INT. GARRETT'S STUDIO - LATER

Cori is lying on her side across the settee as
Garrett places a canvas on an easel and gathers
paints and brushes.

He walks over to position a lamp and shines the
light upon her.

> GARRETT
> Are you warm enough?

> CORI
> Do I look cold?

> GARRETT
> I'd say you look radiant.

> CORI
> Isn't the artist supposed to help
> position his model?

> GARRETT
> I'll need to touch you.

> CORI
> Are my legs good like this?

He lifts her ankle and bends her knee forward.
His hand glides along her leg and spreads her
fingers over her thigh. His fingertips hesitate
at her nipples but move to her neck. He tilts
her chin up, then kisses his paintbrush.

> GARRETT
> Perfection. Hold that pose.

INT. GARRETT'S STUDIO - LATER

Cori's eyes look at the branching arms of Daphne.

> CORI
> How do I compare to your Daphne?

                    GARRETT
        Those are signs of a jealous lover.

                    CORI
        How long will this take?

                    GARRETT
        Days. Months. Maybe Years.

Cori slides off the settee and invades his space.

                    GARRETT
        You're to stay over there if -

Cori covers his mouth with her hand. She looks at —

HER PAINTED IMAGE in progress: the dark searing
eyes, naked skin vibrant with colorful shadows,
and a triangle of pubic hair.

                    CORI (O.C.)
        You have me floating above the
        cushions. I like that.

Garrett places his hand on her thigh and pulls
her around. They kiss. She unbuckles his pants.
He kisses her breasts.

                    GARRETT
        Are you sure you want to do this?

                    CORI
        Let them watch.

They fall down onto the folds of the drop cloth.

INT. GARRETT'S STUDIO - LATER

Cori and Garrett are nestled together on the floor.

                    GARRETT
        Moments like this come but once,
        maybe twice in a life, if lucky.

Cori's fingers explore his chest hairs, finding more scars.

                    GARRETT
          Plate glass window.

CLOSE ON Garrett's fingers touching her skin. She too has scars.

                    GARRETT
          Where did these come from?

Cori shakes her head, dismissing them.

The room wavers in a surreal light. There is a hint of other realms and ghosts in the shadows.

                    CORI
          I feel safe here.

INT. MOTOR-HOME, JUNKYARD - SAME

Dover is immobile, body riddled with bullets. Toothpicks are stuck in both eyes.

EXT. GARDEN, GARRETT'S PROPERTY - SAME

Cori, now dressed, meanders through the garden with a mug in her hands, enchanted by the ambience of the night and the rhythmic CLANGING of Garrett's hammer upon metal.

Cori sits. The pond sparkles in the moonlight. Sculptures CHIME in the wind. Nearby, Neptune and his trident RATTLE.

Cori sniffs the air. She sees something within the bushes. It's not an apparition, but Erin, with her throat cut.

                    CORI
          Jesus!

Stunned, she sits back down. Erin emerges as a
ghost to sit across from Cori who drops her mug.
Her eyes follow Erin's foreboding eyes toward
another seated figure. Cori SCREAMS.

>   PICKARD
>   Hello, Corina.

Cori starts to run but is tackled - knocked to
the ground.

INT. DRIVEWAY, GARRETT'S PROPERTY - SAME

Cori is shoved from behind by Pickard who holds
a semi-automatic pistol.

>   PICKARD
>   You've been avoiding me. Why?

She doesn't reply. He smacks her head with the
gun, grabs the neck of her sweater and pulls her
around to face him.

>   PICKARD
>   Are you malfunctioning?

>   CORI
>   I don't know what you're talking -

Pickard KNOCKS her to the gravel.

>   PICKARD
>   Don't force me to hurt you. Get up!

INT. GARRETT'S STUDIO - LATER

Martino finishes binding Garrett to a chair with
duct tape as Pickard KICKS a chair toward the
forge.

>   PICKARD
>   Her too. Put her over there.

                    GARRETT
What is it you want?

                    PICKARD
I knew you'd have to factor into this
equation, Garrett.

                    GARRETT
Sensitive military data is involved,
that's all I know.

Pickard STABS a toothpick into Garrett's shoulder.

                    PICKARD
Wrong. A device that will render <u>all</u>
military powers useless.

                    CORI
I found it in my purse. I -

                    PICKARD
Of course it was in your purse!

                    CORI
I buried it near the road.

                    PICKARD
What road?

                    CORI
What is it?

Pickard grabs her by the hair and SLAPS her.

                    PICKARD
Snap out of it!

Cori sees the ghost of Stikes standing by the
studio door.

Pickard removes his coat and hangs it on a
chair. He scowls at Martino eating from a bag of
pretzels. He regards the sculptures.

                  PICKARD
Not bad, Garrett. Daphne, there. To
me she always exemplified the frigid
bitch. Apollo was inept. Trust me, I
would have found a way to fuck her.
This must be Tantalus. I too hate
being kept from what I want. Let me
end his suffering.

He grabs a sledge hammer and SMASHES the head.

                  PICKARD
What I'm here for is a biochemical
weapon. It detonates and releases a
pathogen. It's very deadly. Like me.

                  GARRETT
A toxin like that could destroy all
life, including your own, Pickard.

Garrett keeps glancing toward the door.

                  PICKARD
The cavalry ain't coming.

He picks up an iron bar, swings and WALLOPS it
into Redemption. He JABS the bar into hot coals.
He pauses at the portrait of Cori, then walks
over to grab the neck of her sweater.

                  PICKARD
What have you been doing here?

He flips open his knife and CUTS her sweater
down the front. He cups one of her breasts
possessively, as if measuring it, then pinches
one of her nipples, twisting. She SCREAMS.

                  PICKARD
Are you forgetting? These are mine.

He walks over to Garrett, inserts a knife into
his nostril.

                    PICKARD
     I'm not a patient man. I recommend
     you tell me where it's hiding.

                    CORI
     He doesn't know! I buried it in the
     woods. Before I got here.

                    PICKARD
     Convince me.

                    CORI
     I'll have to show you.

                    PICKARD
                (laughs)
     Miss no-show now wants to show us.

He tosses insulated gloves at Martino and nods
at the bar.

                    CORI
     What are you going to do?

                    MARTINO
     Do you like being pretty?

                    GARRETT
     For God's sake, she's telling the
     truth! She told me too. She hid it
     about fifty yards off the highway!

                    PICKARD
     And she said you didn't know a thing.
     Give Cori a little spank.

                    CORI
     Don't! Please don't.

She SCREAMS as Martino brands her shoulder.

                    PICKARD
     You're a little liar.

Fighting the pain, she furiously shakes her head.

                    PICKARD
          Why don't I believe you?

                    CORI
          Because you're an idiot!

She instantly regrets saying it. Pickard grabs
her chin.

                    PICKARD
          Careless words are costly.

Pickard puts on gloves. He grabs the hot iron.
Cori panics. She tries to stand. Martino KNOCKS
her back down. Pickard rotates the glowing tip
before her eyes.

                    PICKARD
          Is this helping you to remember?
          Maybe I'll tickle your nose?

                    GARRETT
          You coward! Leave her alone!

Pickard redirects his anger at Garrett, RIPPING
apart his T-shirt. He sets the bar on his chest.
Garrett CRIES out.

                    PICKARD
          How does it feel being a hero?
          I thought I killed you in Madrid. But
          you just keep coming back.

                    GARRETT
          I retired. Opted out of all this.

                    PICKARD
          Looks to me like you stepped back
          into it. I warned you.

CLOSE ON Cori, intensely listening, taking it in.

> GARRETT
> What's your plan? To kill us all?

He JAMS the bar back in the forge. He grabs
metal shears.

> PICKARD
> Picture this. An artist who is dying
> to paint and sculpt. But he has no
> fingers. And he lives with a once
> beautiful woman who, alas, has become
> tragically disfigured.

Garrett closes his fingers into fists behind the
chair that he's duct-taped to.

> GARRETT
> It's what I'd expect a coward to do.

> PICKARD
> I dislike that word. I'm going to
> teach Special Ops here not to use
> that word. Pull down his pants.

> MARTINO
> Jeez, I'm not going to -

> PICKARD
> Do it!

Cori, horrified, squirms to get free. Pickard
kicks and KNOCKS her chair over. Her head
STRIKES the cement floor.

The BLOW to Cori's head triggers a change, an
AWARENESS.

> PICKARD (O.C.)
> Relax, Cor, when I'm finished, he
> won't want to fuck you anyway.

Pickard places Garrett's small finger between
the shears.

                    PICKARD
          Guess what I snip off next?

                    CORI
          Stop it! Don't!

Garrett writhes in AGONY, losing consciousness.

Cori fights with renewed energy to free herself.

                    CORI (V.O)
          God, I did this. This is my fault.

Martino CAUTERIZES the stub of the severed
finger with the iron. Pickard LAUGHS and snips
the shears in Garrett's face.

                    CORI
          You bastard! We need to talk! Now!

Pickard and Martino pause, break into LAUGHTER.

                    CORI
          Harm him or me again and you will
          never - I swear it, Jimmy - never
          know where I buried that device!

Pickard grabs her hair, lifts her head up.

                    PICKARD
          Who the hell am I talking to?

                    CORI
          Whoever you want me to be. Okay?

                    PICKARD
          Cut the bitch.

                    MARTINO
          Cut her?

                    PICKARD
          Loose.

INT. GARRETT'S STUDIO - LATER

Garrett is pale with sweat. Cori averts her eyes.

Her wrists are tied together in front, wrapped with duct tape. Pickard shoves her forward.

>   PICKARD
>   Show me. He stays with loverboy.

>   CORI
>   He's not my lover.

>   PICKARD
>   Thirty minutes, then more of his
>   fingers start coming off.

>   CORI
>   We'll need more time.

>   PICKARD
>   Why do you care? Move it!

Pickard winks at Garrett before SLAMMING an iron bar into Daphne.

>   GARRETT
>   (teeth clenched)
>   Confirms it. You can only destroy.

Pickard lunges at Garrett. Cori intervenes.

>   CORI
>   Forget him. Let's get this over.

>   PICKARD
>   Consider yourself lucky, Garrett.

>   CORI
>   I need a jacket or something.

>   PICKARD
>   No, your package is perfect for me.

INT. PICKARD'S MERCEDES, DIRT ROAD - NIGHT

Pickard lights a cigarette, grins, and studies
Cori, his passenger, with her arms pressed to
her chest for warmth. She glares back at him to
match his intensity.

                    PICKARD
          You see me as this ugly monster.

                    CORI
          Just a monster.

He LAUGHS, blows smoke at her.

                    PICKARD
          I missed you.

                    CORI
          I pity you.

                    PICKARD
          Did I surprise you back there?

                    CORI
          I knew you'd be coming.

                    PICKARD
          You deviated from our plan.

                    CORI
          Not intentionally. A car hit me. I
          blacked out. And I panicked. My mind,
          it isn't working right.

                    PICKARD
          God, our father, should have never
          implanted his ambitions upon us.
                    (at Cori)
          Our creed. I want to hear it.

                    CORI
          Know who to eliminate.

                    PICKARD
        Exactly. Same rationale used to kill
        you. Which has made you special.

Cori looks away, trying to make sense of his words.

                    CORI
        It's around the next bend.

Cori senses something and turns her head to be
SHOCKED by —

Naught seated in the back seat. Transparent.
Luminescent. He has a fiery aura, a defiant smile.

Pickard's POV: (first time we see it and it's)
HELLISH, his distorted view of the world. He
regards Naught, then Cori.

                    PICKARD
        I see him too. He means shit to me.

Cori is unable to hide her shock.

                    PICKARD
        I made him into a permanent spook.

He swipes his arm backwards. Naught's ghostly
image disperses like smoke.

                    PICKARD
        Regenerative energy. It's the dirty
        little secret of our genome. We're
        not this God-given master-fucking
        code of perfection. No. Life is too
        messy. We're composed of mostly DNA
        junk. Parasitic scribblings. With
        viral hangers-on. Useless shit.

FLASHBACK: CORI RECEIVING AN INJECTION FROM NAUGHT.

Cori silently reacts with horror at this memory.

                    PICKARD (V.O.)
          I'll credit the old man with one
          thing. We are too complicated.

Pickard flicks cigarette ashes out the window.

                    PICKARD
          He was attempting to clean us up.
          Give us a genetic worming.
                    (at Cori)
          Hey, you didn't really think I was
          going to scar your face, did you?

                    CORI
          No. You were just angry.

                    PICKARD
          Damn right. And our father, who art
          now in hell, deserved what he got.
          For making us all into his god-damned
          guinea pigs.

Cori tries to bolster a facade of calm defiance.

                    CORI
          I would have killed him too.

                    PICKARD
                    (circumspect)
          Maybe. We see the world alike, you
          and me. That's unique. Not so bad.

                    CORI
          Except for all the ghosts. Why?

                    PICKARD
                    (laughs)
          Fuck, Cor, for one so smart you sure
          are stupid sometimes. Think about it.
          We've become the main event. End of
          civilization and the world as we know
          it at stake. The release of a lethal
          pandemic is bound to draw a crowd.

Cori forces a smile. She struggles to twist and
undo the duct tape binding her wrists.

                    CORI
          Take this tape off. Pull over here.

Pickard STOPS in the middle of the road, grabs
her by the hair and DRAGS her across the seats
as he steps outside.

                    PICKARD
          You didn't really expect me to
          believe you'd lie down and be this
          good little lamb, did you, Cor?

She TOPPLES to the dirt. His cigarette sparks
beside her.

                    PICKARD
          Get up. Show me.

EXT. FOREST, GARRETT'S PROPERTY - SAME

A flashlight cuts through the darkness. It
shines upon the sculpture of a NYMPH, minus its
golf club in the leaves.

A GUST of wind is heard, followed by the sound
of a WAILING girl.

                    PICKARD
          What the hell was that?
               (at the nymph)
          And who the fuck are you?

                    CORI
          I buried it under her foot.

                    PICKARD
          Fetch it.

With her wrists bound, Cori drops to her knees,
removes the device and stands.

Pickard uses a pocket scanner to analyze the
chemical components within. He takes possession
of the device, drops it in his pocket.

>   PICKARD
>   Verified. Detonator. Completes the
>   package. Now, back to that casino.

Pickard grins and reaches for her breasts. She
backs away.

>   PICKARD
>   Hey, don't forget, Cor, I'm you're
>   ticket out of here. So behave.

Cori follows him and glances back at the NYMPH.

CLOSE ON its ball-bearing eyes expressing shock.

>   CORI
>   Don't you want his gold?

Pickard stops.

>   CORI
>   Garrett discovered gold.

>   PICKARD
>   Bullshit. I would've known that.

>   CORI
>   Stikes told me. Garrett bought this
>   dump to keep a low profile.

From her pocket she removes the gold nugget.
Pickard takes hold of it, weighing both the gold
and her for the truth.

>   PICKARD
>   You're lying.

A gust of wind FLUTTERS through her hair.

                    CORI
Fine. Don't believe me. Your loss.

                    PICKARD
Loverboy is losing more fingers.

                    CORI
I don't really care. I was using him.
Are you going to kill me too?

                    PICKARD
          (amused by her)
It's a strange world. We're this
by-product of conflicting genes.
So many choices. Like who to kill.

                    CORI
I'm not lying. I buried money under
those rocks. And there is gold.

                    PICKARD
Show me.

Cori knocks over the rocks and pulls up the
plastic bag of money she buried. Pickard grabs
it from her and grins.

                    PICKARD
Almost makes me want to fuck you.

                    CORI
Wow, is that next, you rape me out of
gratitude?

                    PICKARD
          (laughs)
You think I'd actually fuck my own
sister. Shit, Cori. You gotta draw a
line somewhere.

                    CORI
          (horrified)
I'm not your — no. No!

                    PICKARD
Get a grip. Let's vacate this dump.
There's still time to release that
pathogen before the conference ends.
Then it's home to the Immortal Tyger.

The NAME triggers a memory.

                              SMASH CUT TO:

AERIAL VIEW OF A SUPERYACHT ANCHORED OFF AN
ISLAND, PANNING CLOSER TO SEE "IMMORTAL TYGER"
PAINTED ACROSS ITS SIDE, THEN CLOSER TO REVEAL
CORI SUNBATHING ON ITS LUXURIOUS UPPER DECK.

                                  BACK TO:

                    CORI
There's a key.

Pickard stops, puzzled by her.

                    CORI
Inside, wrapped around the money.
          (forceful)
The key to his safe. There's over a
million in gold. I'm on your side,
Jimmy! I've done this before!

                    PICKARD
Most of that shit is manufactured
memories. But you earned your keep.

As he searches the bag Cori KICKS for his groin.
He catches her foot but drops the gun and money.
She rapidly hops off her other foot and KICKS
him backwards.

They scramble for the gun. A bullet FIRES as he
knocks it from her hand. She dives for the golf
club. She swings and CONNECTS the 9 iron into
his knee. She swings again STRIKING his mouth,
crushing his teeth. She dives and grabs the gun.

A car appears with a rotating beacon and a white spotlight. Cori waves her bound hands. She moves toward the vehicle.

                    MALE VOICE
                  (loud speaker)
             Police! Stop right there!

                      CORI
          Help me!

She points at Pickard. His mouth is bloody. He is limping toward her.

                    MALE VOICE
             Drop your weapon! Do it!

                      CORI
          You don't understand, that man -

                    MALE VOICE
             Drop the gun! Now!

Through the glare, she sees another figure who exits the passenger door, holding a gun.

Cori looks back at Pickard who gives a sharp head nod.

                      CORI
             Okay! Okay! I'm dropping it!

She dives and FIRES at the silhouetted figures as Pickard YELLS -

                     PICKARD
          Kill her!

A flurry of BULLETS. Both men by the car are HIT and drop.

Pickard is limping away. She SHOOTS. He staggers and falls.

She starts to go after him then hesitates, runs for the car instead.

INT. POLICE CAR, GARRETT'S PROPERTY - NIGHT

The dead men are not wearing police uniforms.

With her wrists still tied, Cori starts the police car and drives off-road to get around the Mercedes. She drives through brush to return to the road. The car CRASHES into a solid object.

EXT. POLICE CAR, GARRETT'S PROPERTY - SAME

Shaken, Cori exits the car holding the gun. She approaches the object that she has hit. It's a car. Inside are two men with their throats cut.

                    CORI
          God almighty!

EXT. DIRT ROAD, GARRETT'S PROPERTY - SAME

Cori runs clutching the gun to her chest. The moon above the trees show patches of definition. She trips and FALLS. She recovers, gets up and keeps running. The wind is ROARING.

EXT./INT. GARRETT'S ART STUDIO - LATER

Cori peers inside. Garrett is alive, still tied to the chair, his head slumped. A table blocks the view of his hands. Martino stands over him eating pretzels, holding the shears.

                    MARTINO
          Guess this ain't your lucky night.

                    CORI
          Don't move!

                    MARTINO
          Where's James?

141

                    CORI
          Dead like you.

Martino dodges as she FIRES. First bullet RIPS
off part of his ear. Second misses and HITS the
table. He uses Garrett as a shield.

                    MARTINO
          The hell's gotten into you, Cori?

He wildly looks around trying to locate her.

                    MARTINO
          Where'd you go? Stop it, god damn it!

Cori slithers on her stomach behind the sculptures.

She surprises Martino by rising behind a damaged
Daphne and FIRES the gun, hitting Martino in the
head. He collapses, dead.

INT. GARRETT'S STUDIO - LATER

Fearing the worst, Cori approaches Garrett. His
fingers are intact, all but one. Her naked torso
has scratches, her face is filthy, hair matted.

She PULLS the duct tape off his mouth.

                    GARRETT
               (hoarse)
          You're a beautiful sight.

                    CORI
          I know.

INT. GARRETT'S STUDIO - LATER

Cori's body begins to shake as she uses scissors
to cut the tape off her wrists.

She then cuts away the tape binding Garrett.

                    GARRETT
Where's Pickard?

                     CORI
I knocked out his teeth.

Garrett removes a toothpick from his shoulder.

                    GARRETT
With what?

                     CORI
Golf club. Your nymph's flute. Then I
shot him. He's dead, I think.

She averts her eyes from his severed finger on
the floor.

Garrett retrieves the guns, hands one to her.
From a closet he removes a T-shirt and sweatshirt and hands them to her.

                     CORI
I was cold. Thank you.

Garrett helps her put on the sweatshirt.

                    GARRETT
We need to make sure he's dead.

                     CORI
Lots of bodies on your property.
Those cowboys, they're dead too.
Inside a car beside the road.
          (grabs his arm)
I may have killed two policemen.

                    GARRETT
When?

                     CORI
They drove in, and - I wasn't sure.
So I shot first.

                    GARRETT
        CIA, maybe. We'll check it out.

                     CORI
        I'm - Pickard's sister.

                    GARRETT
        What? Come on, let's hurry.

EXT. JUNKYARD, GARRETT'S PROPERTY - LATER

Garrett, with a flashlight, moves with Cori
between the cars.

                     CORI
        Where are we going?

                    GARRETT
        I need to find out something.

The motor home has been doused with gasoline.
The door FLAPS in the wind against its frame.

INT. MOTOR-HOME, JUNKYARD - SAME

Briggs and Dover resemble a still-life portrait
of a massacre.

EXT. DRIVEWAY, GARRETT'S HOUSE - MOMENTS LATER

Cori stops Garrett as they move toward his truck.

                     CORI
        Tell me the truth. Did you know?

                    GARRETT
        Know what?

                     CORI
        That Pickard - he's - my brother?

                    GARRETT
        You don't sound sure.

CUT TO:

A ROAR from Pickard's Mercedes as it accelerates toward them.

Garrett is STRUCK - thrown against the fountain.

Cori leaps onto the porch to avoid the Mercedes that CRASHES into it. She FIRES at Pickard. The windshield SHATTERS. Her gun is now empty.

As Garrett stands, Pickard opens the car door and SHOOTS him twice with his derringer. Garrett collapses.

Cori throws her gun at him as Pickard reloads his derringer.

                    CORI
          You piece of shit! I hate you!

Cori runs and hides behind the statue of Neptune.

Pickard limps toward her.

She removes her sweatshirt and throws it onto the sculpture to distract him as she runs away.

A bullet GRAZES her side. She DIVES into the pond.

EXT. POND/ISLAND, GARRETT'S PROPERTY - SAME

A bullet HITS the water as Cori surfaces. The next one GRAZES the side of her head. She swims around the island.

                    PICKARD
          You won't eshcape me. Wanna play
          ruff, Cor? Now you die!

He stops to listen, spits blood, steps in the pond, and lowers himself into the water.

EXT. POND/ISLAND, GARRETT'S PROPERTY - LATER

Pickard emerges from the water and crawls across
the island. From behind a rock, he sees her head
in the water. He lunges and GRABS her hair.

>   PICKARD
>   Caught you!

He DRAGS Cori by the neck onto land, KNEES her
stomach to immobilize her, STRIKES her face,
then SPITS blood on her. He removes his knife
and places the blade to her crotch.

>   PICKARD
>   I'm gonna cutcha shlow, starting
>   between your legs up to your titsh.

Cori looks at the moon GLARING like a blind eye.
The wind is GUSTING. Trees CREAKING. Sculptures
CLANGING. It sounds like the GATES OF HELL.

>   CORI
>   (strangled voice)
>   God. Save me.

>   PICKARD
>   That's it, pway for a miracle.

A light FLARES across Pickard's face.

He looks up and sees a glowing man with arms
outstreched as if crucified. It's Stikes holding
a cue stick behind his neck, with a grim head
shake that says: "I am not letting you do that."

>   PICKARD
>   (recovers, laughs)
>   Phuck you, dead man. Watch me.

Terrified and delirious, Cori envisions NEPTUNE
coming toward them, holding his trident, walking
across the water and rising onto land.

                    PICKARD
No one phucks with me and lives -

Pickard's eyes widen. His stranglehold freezes and
loosens. Cori pushes him away. He falls to the side.

Neptune's trident is stuck in Pickard's back.

Garrett is soaking wet, standing over the body.
He collapses beside Cori. He touches her face.

                    CORI
I thought he'd killed you.

                    GARRETT
First bullet went through my side.
Second hit my belt. Hell of a punch.

Shaken and afraid, Cori stares at Pickard's body.

                    CORI
You said you were a pacifist.

Garrett notices blood trailing down her face.

                    GARRETT
You're hurt.

                    CORI
No. I hurt people. I hurt you.

                    GARRETT
Cori, I'm okay. It's okay.

                    CORI
          (winces)
No, it's not. I'm a horrible person.
I've done awful things. I'm Daphne.
I'm poison!

                    GARRETT
Calm down. Cori, I -

She pushes him away.

>   CORI
>   I'm a thief. A liar. I steal. I would
>   have stolen all your gold.

>   GARRETT
>   There is no gold. Only my heart.

>   CORI
>   Don't tempt me.

She suddenly remembers something urgent. She
struggles to sit up and search through Pickard's
drenched clothing.

>   GARRETT
>   What are you looking for?

Cori finds the cylindrical device in this pants.

CLOSE ON - red LCD numbers blinking: 3:33 ...
3:33 ... 3:33 ...

>   CORI
>   Shit. It's activated. He called this
>   thing the detonator.

>   GARRETT
>   The numbers aren't moving.

>   CORI
>   It wasn't showing numbers before.

>   GARRETT
>   There's nothing here to detonate.

>   SMASH CUT TO:

FLASHBACK OF CORI INSPECTING THE SURGICAL SCARS
BENEATH HER BREASTS IN THE BATHROOM.

>   BACK TO:

EXT. GARRETT'S PROPERTY, POND/ISLAND - SAME

> CORI
> It's me.

> GARRETT
> What is?

> CORI
> He put explosives inside of me.

She drops the device and pulls her knees up to her chest. She hugs herself, shivering.

> GARRETT
> What are you talking about?

> CORI
> I kill people. That's what I do.

CLOSE ON the device continuing to BLINK: 3:33.

> CORI
> I'm the fucking jackpot. He made me into a suicide bomb! That bastard!

She recoils as Garrett touches her shoulder.

> CORI
> Don't touch me. Leave! Run!

> GARRETT
> You're not making any sense.

> CORI
> Don't you get it? It's inside me - my breasts. The explosives.

Garrett is stunned, then -

> GARRETT
> Maybe not. It could be the formula.

Cori's eyes narrow, demanding to know - WHAT?

                    GARRETT
          Your father swore under oath he
          destroyed everything, the formula
          too. But I can't believe he would.
          It was too precious a discovery.

CLOSE ON Cori's eyes as they close.

DISSOLVE TO darkness as water LAPS the shore.

                    CORI (V.O)
          Oh, God. I did work for my brother.
          I _am_ a criminal. Trained to steal and
          kill. No. I was sent to infiltrate
          his operation. Doing espionage work.

                    GARRETT
          As a CIA operative?

                    CORI
          I don't know what I am anymore.

Cori flinches when he touches her, then allows
him to stroke her hair and neck, bringing her
closer and calming her like a wild animal.

                    GARRETT
          You're a mess.

Her body shudders, shivering, as she sobs.

                    GARRETT
          And, I love you.

She shakes her head but accepts his compassion.

                    GARRETT
          Your father found a way to unlock
          dormant cells and stimulate our
          cranial nerves. The gifts we received
          have regenerative powers.

Cori pushes away to look at him.

                    CORI
          You mean the opposite of death.

                    GARRETT
          We won't be dying anytime soon.

He redirects her eyes on Pickard, her brother.

                    GARRETT
          How do you think I survived that
          beating? I was as good as dead.

                    CORI
          Then that means. He'll live?

                    GARRETT
          We're safe. For the time being.

                    CORI
          No. We're not. We're cursed. Cursed
          with life. Everlasting life!

                    GARRETT
          Unless incinerated. Cremated.

                    CORI
          We need to act fast and burn him.

Cori is helped up by Garrett.

The horizon has a faint glow from an approaching
sun coming into view.

The apparitions of people are transforming into
reeds and trees that border the pond.

The wind has receded into a light breeze. A bird
is heard TRILLING in the morning silence.

Cori reaches down and grabs a handful of dirt.
She THROWS it onto Pickard.

> CORI
> You want to know what makes us human
> - what separates us from all the
> other stupid animals?
> (furious)
> Our ability to lie.

> GARRETT
> Animals lie.

> CORI
> No they don't.

> GARRETT
> Sure they do. They'll sometimes feign
> death to survive.

Cori looks down at Pickard. His presence is like a dormant anaconda. She KICKS him in the head.

> CORI
> Not the same.

The sky RUMBLES, sounding as if the world is GYRATING and about to come apart. A helicopter appears over the trees.

> CORI
> That's natural deceit. Humans lie
> with words. We deceive ourselves.

A floodlight shines down on Garrett's house. The beam of white light moves across the property.

The searchlight finds the pond, island, then -

CLOSE ON PICKARD'S EYES AS THEY BEGIN TO OPEN.

SMASH CUT TO:

INT. LAB ROOM, U.C. BERKELEY - NIGHT (FLASHBACK)

Cori lunges upright. Her eyes are wide from shock.

Her body is on a laboratory table hooked to a
multitude of wires and monitoring equipment.

Naught is raptly observing her behavior.

> NAUGHT
> Where were did you go, Cori? Quick,
> before the memory passes. Tell us
> what you envisioned! What happened?

Cori is disoriented, unable to speak. Eleven
college students surround her, including Dover,
Stikes, Alex, Garrett, and -

Her view shifts to lock onto her brother, whose
face has a wicked, as if prescient, smirk.

INSERT: PICKARD'S FACE, PRESENT DAY AT DAWN,
BODY IMMOBILE, A TRIDENT STUCK IN HIS BODY.

Cori collapses back onto the laboratory table.

> DOVER (V.O.)
> Her vital signs are dropping.

> NAUGHT (V.O.)
> No one panic.

> STIKES (V.O.)
> Oh, fuck. She's flat-lined. Fuck!

> GARRETT (V.O.)
> Cori, don't die. Can you hear me?

> NAUGHT (V.O.)
> She can hear us. Everyone stay calm.

BACK TO:

INT. MOTOR HOME, JUNKYARD - DAWN, PRESENT DAY

Briggs is dead. Dover begins to move and GROAN.

EXT. POND/ISLAND, OVERVIEW - SAME MORNING

The FLOODLIGHT finds Cori looking down at -

Pickard with the trident stuck in his back, his body on its side, head turned, eyes wide open, looking up at her with a bloody toothless grin.

Garrett SHOUTS to be heard over the HELICOPTER.

>   GARRETT (V.O.)
> This world. I was praying for love.
> I had no idea God would send me you.

>   CORI
> He sent you thorns, not roses.

Her sarcasm warms as the white searchlight moves off them and sunlight shines on her face.

>   GARRETT (V.O.)
> God sends you what you need. So, I
> guess, I needed you.

Cori's face slowly transforms into a painting.

>   CORI (V.O.)
> I'm dangerous.

>   GARRETT (V.O.)
> We'll manage.

>   CORI (V.O.)
> I can't even trust myself.

>   GARRETT (V.O.)
> I trust you.

>   CORI (V.O.)
> We could be annihilated any second.

>   GARRETT (V.O.)
> Or live.

TITLE: NINE YEARS LATER

EXT. GARRETT'S PROPERTY, OVERVIEW - SUNNY DAY

Viewed from above, the island, pond, house,
junkyard, and trees diminish. Children are heard
LAUGHING and SWIMMING in the pond.

PAN TO a beautiful blue sky with massive white
clouds, yellow-rimmed and purple-shadowed.

Everything dissolves as the camera film heats
and burns and bubbles into multiple colors.

FREEZE on this ABSTRACTION.

>   CORI (V.O.)
> Van Gogh was right. God can't be
> judged from this world. Life is a
> sketch we'll never understand.
>   (beat)
> And maybe that's good.

                              FADE OUT:

        THE END

When the stars threw down their spears

And water'd heaven with its tears:

Did he smile his work to me?

Did he who made the Lamb make me?

— William Blake , The Tyger

www.ingramcontent.com/pod-product-compliance
Lightning Source LLC
Chambersburg PA
CBHW071257130626
46556CB00003B/1349